𝒥𝒲𝒶
12/6/8?

THE SHADOW GREW STILL.
IT WAS THE GIRL ...

Instantly, Longarm flung himself about and brought up his revolver, shoving the bore up into Frida's startled face.

"Take me with you," Frida pleaded.

"And just why should I do that? You're a fine cook, I must admit. But you're baggage that would slow me down, and that's a fact."

"Please! You must take me." She moved suddenly closer to him. "You won't regret it, I promise you! Let me show you . . ."

Also in the LONGARM series
from Jove

LONGARM
LONGARM ON THE BORDER
LONGARM AND THE AVENGING ANGELS
LONGARM AND THE WENDIGO
LONGARM IN THE INDIAN NATION
LONGARM AND THE LOGGERS
LONGARM AND THE HIGHGRADERS
LONGARM AND THE NESTERS
LONGARM AND THE HATCHET MEN
LONGARM AND THE MOLLY MAGUIRES
LONGARM AND THE TEXAS RANGERS
LONGARM IN LINCOLN COUNTY
LONGARM IN THE SAND HILLS
LONGARM IN LEADVILLE
LONGARM ON THE DEVIL'S TRAIL
LONGARM AND THE MOUNTIES
LONGARM AND THE BANDIT QUEEN
LONGARM ON THE YELLOWSTONE
LONGARM IN THE FOUR CORNERS
LONGARM AT ROBBER'S ROOST
LONGARM AND THE SHEEPHERDERS
LONGARM AND THE GHOST DANCERS
LONGARM AND THE TOWN TAMER
LONGARM AND THE RAILROADERS
LONGARM ON THE OLD MISSION TRAIL
LONGARM AND THE DRAGON HUNTERS
LONGARM AND THE RURALES
LONGARM ON THE HUMBOLDT
LONGARM ON THE BIG MUDDY
LONGARM SOUTH OF THE GILA
LONGARM IN NORTHFIELD
LONGARM AND THE GOLDEN LADY
LONGARM AND THE LAREDO LOOP
LONGARM AND THE BOOT HILLERS
LONGARM AND THE BLUE NORTHER
LONGARM ON THE SANTA FE
LONGARM AND THE STALKING CORPSE
LONGARM AND THE COMANCHEROS

TABOR EVANS

LONGARM

AND THE DEVIL'S RAILROAD

A JOVE BOOK

LONGARM AND THE DEVIL'S RAILROAD

Copyright © 1981 by Jove Publications, Inc.

All rights reserved. No part of this publication may be reproduced or transmitted in any form or by any means, electronic or mechanical, including photocopy, recording, or any information storage and retrieval system, without permission in writing from the publisher.

Requests for permission to make copies of any part of the work should be mailed to: Permissions, Jove Publications, Inc., 200 Madison Avenue, New York, NY 10016

First Jove edition published December 1981

First printing

Printed in the United States of America

Jove books are published by Jove Publications, Inc., 200 Madison Avenue, New York, NY 10016

LONGARM
AND THE
DEVIL'S RAILROAD

Chapter 1

His upper lip fully lathered, a straight-edge razor in his right hand, Longarm leaned his face close to the cracked mirror resting on top of the dresser—and cursed.

He didn't want to do it. The thought of shaving off his longhorn mustache filled him with dismay.

But then, abruptly, he shrugged and began scraping at his upper lip. It was too late to think this over now; he had already snipped off most of the mustache anyway, and besides, he told himself ruefully, it served him right for making his face so damn familiar to so many hardcases west of the Mississippi.

The operation completed, Longarm dipped his big hands into the pan of water sitting in front of the mirror and washed the lather off his face. Then he toweled himself dry and shrugged into his black cotton shirt, over which he pulled a buttonless black leather vest. From the top of the dresser he plucked a black eyepatch and tied it over his left eye.

He didn't like the one-sided view it forced on him, but he had practiced shooting while wearing the patch for the past week, and he was confident it would not hinder his gunplay too much.

He clapped a black, flat-crowned Stetson on his head and began pacing back and forth across the cabin's rough plank flooring, shooting an occasional glance at the mirror as he did so. Faking a limp, he was soon moving with a kind of sinister, dipping stride. At last, satisfied that his transformation was complete, Longarm pulled up and nodded grimly at his reflection. Deputy U.S. Marshal Custis Long was now the infamous Wolf Caulder, notorious as a one-man execution squad and for the last few years a ruthless but efficient robber of isolated banks and small trunk railroads.

Stopping before his cot, Longarm pulled it away from the wall, then snatched up the carpetbag resting on it. Inside the carpetbag were his brown suit, gray flannel shirt, and cross-draw rig. A separate bundle of oil-soaked rags contained his Colt Model T .44-40, along with his Ingersoll watch and its deadly watch fob: the double-barreled .44 derringer that had pulled him out of so many deadly scrapes in the past. He would miss both weapons, he knew. But they too, it seemed, were almost as well known as that longhorn mustache of his.

He had already pried up the floorboards under the cot and hollowed out a small depression in the earth beneath them. Into this small grave he placed the weapons and the carpetbag, with his snuff-brown Stetson alongside them, then replaced the floorboards. With a heavy rock he nailed the boards solidly back into place, pushed the cot back against the wall, turned, and left the cabin.

Longarm swung up into the saddle of his waiting mount, a broad-chested roan gelding. He had selected this mount carefully, then had ridden it flat-out for days through this rugged country. Only when he was certain that the big, handsome animal was equal to its appearance and had the endurance it would need, had he allowed himself to purchase it.

2

He would need such a mount if he was going to be able to pull off this desperate gamble.

It was close to noon when Longarm reached Ridge Town, Idaho. Before he rode in, he held up for a moment in the shade of a cottonwood to look the town over. He knew the town well enough, having visited it twice within the past week. What he wanted now was to make sure there was no unusual activity. He had chosen midweek, a Wednesday, and as a result the town was just as quiet as Longarm had hoped it would be. The last thing he wanted was to find himself in the middle of another Northfield debacle, like the one that had decimated the James gang.

He watched the nondescript town bake silently in the noonday sun for a while, then urged his horse on out from under the cottonwood, rode past the water tower, crossed the plank bridge, and continued on down Market Street to the First National Bank, a wood frame building with a high false front. Dismounting in front of the hitch rail, he dropped the roan's reins over the rail, ducked under it, and mounted the wooden sidewalk. He looked quickly up and down the street, patted the Smith & Wesson that rested on his right hip in its flapless army holster, then pushed into the bank.

The bank appeared to have no customers. There were two cashier's windows. At one of them Longarm saw a clerk with a green eyeshade counting out greenbacks. Drawing his revolver, Longarm walked up to the clerk and thrust its muzzle into his face. Then he pulled a pillowcase from his belt and slapped it down across the counter.

"Get that safe open, mister," Longarm told the clerk. "And fill this here pillowcase."

But the clerk was in no condition to cooperate. Wide-eyed, his mouth working in fear, he thrust both hands into the air and stumbled backward, the greenbacks he had been counting fluttering down about him to the floor. Another clerk—a small, round-faced individual coming out of a small office beside the vault—took one look at Longarm and flung his arms up also.

"Hurry up!" Longarm barked. "Get that safe open!"

3

At once the second clerk knelt before the huge vault and, with shaking fingers, spun the tumblers and pulled open the safe. Impatient, Longarm vaulted over the counter, snatched up the pillowcase, and thrust it at the clerk.

"Who—who the hell are you?" the round-faced clerk demanded, as he took the pillowcase from Longarm.

"I ain't Jesse James," Longarm said, "if that'll make you feel any better. Name's Caulder, Wolf Caulder. But I like money just as much as Jesse does. So get in there and fill this up!"

The man swallowed unhappily and hurried into the vault. In a moment he returned with a bulging pillowcase and handed it to Longarm. Longarm took it, limped swiftly through the low gate, and hurried toward the door. Before he reached it, however, a gun roared behind him and a chunk of the door sill exploded in his face.

He looked back and saw that the clerk with the green eyeshade had a huge Colt in both his hands and was pulling it down to get off another shot. Longarm flung a bullet at the man, then ducked out of the bank, cursing. The shots had already roused the sleeping town. From a hardware store across the street, three men bolted, one of them carrying a rifle.

Longarm snatched up his mount's reins and vaulted into the saddle. Wheeling the roan about, he fired at the three men across the street, then clapped spurs to his roan and headed for the plank bridge at a full gallop, the deadly rattle of rifle fire erupting behind him.

He glanced back.

The three men had mounted up and were being joined by two others, one of them Sheriff Dinwiddee. As the five riders swept down the street after Longarm, two more joined them, throwing lead as they came. Longarm clattered over the wooden bridge, swept past the cottonwood, and let his mount have its head. At once he felt the animal's powerful legs increase their stride.

Once more he looked back at his pursuers. The small posse had not yet reached the water tower. Even as he watched, he saw still other riders joining up, causing a momentary milling about as the posse waited for them. Longarm smiled, turned back around, and patted his mount's neck, urging him on with soft words of encouragement. The animal responded with a second powerful surge as Longarm glanced ahead of him at the dim, spectacular ramparts of the Bitterroots. He was certain, now, that he would reach them safely.

Two hours later, his horse cropping the meadow grass behind him, Longarm watched the posse winding its way up the narrow draw toward him. When he judged that it was time, he returned to his horse, led it over to a small sapling, then tied its reins securely to the sapling's trunk. He did not want the firing of his Sharps to spook the horse. He could not afford to lose it now.

Withdrawing the Sharps from its saddle scabbard, he clambered up onto the shelf he had selected a week before. Sitting down crosslegged, he unbuckled his cartridge belt and set it down on the grass beside him. Half the cartridges on the belt were .50 caliber, center-fire. He brought up the Sharps, levered the trigger guard, which opened the chamber, and slipped one of the .50-caliber slugs into it. Pulling shut the trigger guard, he wedged the rifle's stock into his left shoulder and sighted carefully down the barrel at the lead rider, Sheriff Dinwiddee. He judged the distance at just under six hundred yards.

He had already cut himself a shooting stick. He now put the rifle down and stuck the stick into the ground. The stick was not very steady, however, and he had some difficulty finding a stable enough spot to plant the stick—but at last he was ready. He rested the barrel of the Sharps in the crotch of the stick and began to track the sheriff once again.

The distance was close to five hundred yards by this time. He pulled the hammer of the Sharps back gently, tucked the stock securely into his shoulder, aimed, took a deep breath—and squeezed the trigger.

The stock dug into his shoulder as the Sharps recoiled, its detonation filling the narrow valley with a reverberation that seemed to increase in intensity with each echo. Longarm saw Dinwiddee pull up suddenly as a chunk of granite from the wall over his head splintered down upon him.

Chuckling, Longarm reloaded, sighted carefully a second time, and fired. This time the turf in front of the second horseman exploded. In a moment the posse was milling in the narrow draw, trying to decide where the shots were coming from. Longarm reloaded rapidly and fired a third time. A branch just above a posse member galloping up to the sheriff snapped off and crashed down before him. His horse reared almost straight back, flinging the rider to the ground.

So far, so good, Longarm told himself. It had been a long time since he had used a Sharps, but it had never failed him before, and it sure as hell was doing the job at this moment. Figuring one more shot would do it, Longarm reloaded, aimed carefully, and fired again. He cut it pretty close this time and saw the lead rider grab for his hat a split second after the slug had ripped it off his head.

Cold sweat beaded on Longarm's forehead. He had not intended to cut it *that* close!

But that last one did the job. The riders whirled about and galloped back down the narrow valley. Before long they were well out of range, and a moment later they were out of sight. A broad smile on his face, Longarm picked up his cartridge belt and slipped down off the shelf and headed for his mount.

It was close to sundown and Longarm, astride his mount, watched the cabin far below him carefully for signs of life. He had been waiting on this ridge for close to an hour and was beginning to lose hope. But the indolence of the more slothful members of the human race was something that never failed to amaze Longarm; he kept his vigil and waited patiently.

At last his patience was rewarded. A lone figure left the cabin carrying something—it looked like a slops jar—and emptied it off the lip of the ridge on which the cabin had been built. Then, scratching his untidy mop of white hair, the fellow returned to the cabin and disappeared inside.

Longarm knew the man.

His name was Cal Short. He used to rob banks, stage-coaches, and anything else handy, and had, as a result, served time in a few of the more notorious prisons of the West. But since his last term he had not raised a bit of dust, and yet was quietly and rapidly getting wealthy as he lazed away his days and nights swilling whiskey in this mean little cabin he had found in the middle of the Bitterroot Mountains.

Satisfied that Short was in the cabin, Longarm relaxed and eased himself out of his saddle and took a long, lazy stretch. So far, everything had gone just as he had planned. Wolf Caulder had just robbed another bank, confirming the fact that he was still at large.

Only Longarm and Marshal Billy Vail knew the truth—that Wolf Caulder had been gunned down by a young Mexican gunslinger in a cantina somewhere south of Chihuahua, Mexico, six months ago. It was only by chance that Vail had discovered this fact, and when he had reported it to Longarm, both men saw in it the chance they had been waiting for all these months.

The moon was up, a ghostly silver dollar sitting on the peaks behind him, when the sound came of many riders galloping up the narrow draw leading to the ridge below. In a moment the posse appeared. Before the horsemen arrived at the cabin, Cal Short appeared in his littered front yard, cradling what looked like a shotgun in his arms.

The posse halted before him. Not a single rider dismounted. Longarm could not hear what was being said, but he could imagine the dialogue. Since everyone in the county knew of Cal Short's past and of his recently acquired affluence, he was naturally the first person they would seek out in their attempt to find Wolf Caulder. After a moment of dickering, Longarm saw two men dismount and move past Cal Short into his cabin.

The search did not take long. The two men left the cabin and mounted up. After a few more words with Short, the posse turned about and rode off, moving this time in the direction of Ridge Town. Longarm waited a decent interval, then mounted up and set his horse walking down the slope toward the cabin.

He did not dismount when he reached the ridge, and made no effort to quiet his approach to the cabin. As expected, the lantern within the cabin winked out suddenly, and a moment later the door opened and a white-haired figure appeared in the doorway. In the cold light of the moon, Longarm caught the gleam of his shotgun's two barrels.

"Okay, mister," Short called out. "Hold it right there. And don't make no moves sudden-like."

"Hadn't intended to."

"Who are you?"

"Wolf Caulder."

The man squinted up at Longarm in the dim light, then moved closer for a better look. Longarm sat his mount quietly and let Short get as close as he wanted.

"Hell, sure enough. You're Wolf Caulder, all right. Eyepatch and all. There was a few men on horseback up here not too long ago, lookin' for you. Seems you robbed the First National Bank in Ridge Town. You must be a rich man all of a sudden. That so?"

"It's getting chilly out here, and I could use a cup of coffee."

Short chuckled. "Guess you could at that," he said. "Light and set a spell. A man with your reputation is always welcome."

"That's what I heard," Longarm said, dismounting.

"You can leave your mount go loose," Short told Longarm. "He can run with my animal in the meadow below. There's always fresh graze and plenty of water."

Longarm nodded and set to work unsaddling the roan. As he busied himself with the cinch, Short told him he would put the coffee on, and walked back into his cabin. Longarm smiled with satisfaction as he lifted the saddle off the roan, then peeled off the sweat-stained saddle blanket.

The plan was working. He had reached the first station on the Devil's Railroad—and he had his ticket already. It was inside that pillowcase he had filled at the bank.

A moment later, after watching the horse kick up its heels as it disappeared into the meadow below, he lugged his saddle toward the cabin's open door, smelling with anticipation the aroma of fresh coffee heavy on the air.

But as he started through the doorway he heard quick, light footsteps behind him and felt the mean bite of a gun barrel prodding him cruelly in his back. Before he could turn, there came a sharp, clear woman's voice whispering to him to keep going without uttering a sound, or she would be forced to shoot him in the back.

Longarm hesitated only a moment, then moved into the cabin. His back to the door, Short was placing a coffeepot on the table. The man suspected nothing, either. With an inward groan, Longarm dropped his saddle on the floor and turned about to face the girl. The big Colt in her right hand did not waver.

He was startled by her beauty and by the icy anger he saw in her dark eyes. All this planning, Longarm thought wearily, and a fool woman mucks it up.

Chapter 2

"Now who the hell might you be, ma'am?" Longarm asked.

"Frida!" Short called out in some exasperation. "Put down that iron and leave Mr. Caulder be! He's come here on business!"

The cold anger in Frida's eyes faded, to be replaced with annoyance. She lowered the Colt with some reluctance. "You mean he ain't with the sheriff?" she asked Short.

"Nope. Far from it, girl." Short cackled happily at Frida's mistake. "Far from it. He's the gent that posse was after. He's just lightened Ridge Town's First National Bank some, that's what!"

Frida shrugged and stuck the barrel of the Colt into her belt. She wore Levi's and a man's blue cotton shirt with the top couple of buttons open. A black bandanna was tied loosely about her neck. Thick curls of auburn hair coiled down from the brim of her battered plains hat. She was

11

tanned to a solid brown, with dark, smoldering eyes, a sharp nose, and an impudent chin.

She filled out her Levi's and shirt right nicely, Longarm noted.

Picking his saddle back up off the floor, Longarm carried it over to a corner of the room, where he dropped it alongside his bedroll. Frida closed the door behind him and chucked the hat off her head, letting it hang down on her back from its chin thong, and walked over to the stove to help Short.

"I got it, Frida," Short told her as he finished dumping the coffee into the pot. Short had started a fire in the stove, and the cabin was filling with the cozy smell of wood burning.

Longarm walked over and sat down at the deal table near the stove, his eyes on Frida. "This here your daughter?" he asked Short.

"Nope," Short said. "Never had the time to get married." The old man glanced with some fondness at Frida. "She just showed up a while ago, like some lost kitten, all muddied and scratched, and her clothes in tatters."

Frida looked across the table at Longarm and smiled slightly. "Cal was nice enough to take me in, Mr. Caulder. Without asking no questions, neither."

"Then I won't ask any," Longarm promised solemnly, returning her smile.

"She won't tell you," Short said, putting the coffee down before his place and Longarm's, then sitting down himself. "So I will. Just to warn you. She worked at one of them honkytonks where the men come in unhappy and kinda wild, and leave sometime later, mighty content and no longer so itchy for a fight, if'n you know what I mean."

"I know what you mean."

"But one young cowpoke didn't know how to say thank you, so Frida had to shoot the son of a bitch low in the belly to teach him some manners. When the damn fool kid up and died on her, she took off, ended up here. Heard about that Devil's Railroad the same as you did."

"Where'd all this happen, Frida?" Longarm asked.

"West of here," Frida replied, getting up from the table

and moving over to the stove to pour herself a cup of coffee.

"She's been here ever since," Short explained happily, "hoping some gent would come along with enough money to get her a ride on that there railroad."

"No luck, huh?" Longarm asked the girl. He was having some difficulty believing a girl like this would have had any trouble at all convincing a man to give her what she would need for the journey.

"Plenty of luck," she replied, returning to the table with her coffee and sitting down. "But all of it bad."

"Frida's a mite choosey," explained Short. "But I don't mind. She keeps these here digs real clean and cooks up a storm. Besides, I ain't never had a daughter—until now, that is."

Short smiled at Frida, revealing a ravaged row of broken and blackened teeth. Frida reached over, somewhat obediently, and squeezed the old man's leathery hand, smiling back at him as she did. Short immediately flushed with pleasure. Longarm could sense at once how much he liked the girl—and how difficult it would be for him to let her go. He wondered if that could have had anything to do with Frida's bad luck.

He looked at Short. "How much is a ticket on this here railroad going to cost me, Short?"

The man became wary; a crafty light gleamed in his eyes as he appraised Longarm. "How much did you say you heisted from that bank?"

"Didn't."

"That's right. You didn't. But I heard. Close to ten thousand."

Frida's eyebrows went up a notch.

Longarm shrugged. "That's close enough, I guess."

"Then it'll cost you two thousand," said Short.

"You're crazy, old man," Longarm snorted. "I'll find my own way out of this country—and for a hell of a lot less."

"Maybe—and maybe not. That posse was real angry, Wolf. They don't look to me like they's gonna let you out of this country without a tussle. Besides, that price includes a lovely boat ride to South America. You ever seen any of them Spanish females they got down there?"

"Two thousand is way out of line, Short."

The old man shrugged. "I ain't allowed to dicker. But I tell you what. When you reach the next fellow on this end, dicker with him."

"And who might that be?"

Once again, Short displayed his ragged grin.

Longarm shrugged. "All right. I'll dicker with him, then."

Short leaned back and smiled craftily. "But meeting him will cost you eight hundred."

Longarm appeared astonished. "For you?"

"Hell, yes. That's my share. I got to live too, don't I?"

Longarm knew it would be wise for him not to agree to Short's cut too readily. It would look a lot more natural to Short if Longarm bargained—and if he kept what they settled on finally out of Short's sweaty grasp until he was in sight of that gent in charge of the next 'station.'

"Five hundred," Longarm drawled. "You'll take that and like it."

"Five hundred?" cried Short angrily.

"You heard me."

Short's eyes narrowed greedily. "Now dammit, mister, I told you. I don't like all this here dickering. Eight hundred, and that's as low as I'm going. And I'm warning you, Caulder. I don't take kindly to them as tries to cheat me outa my fair share."

Longarm reached over and grabbed Short by the shirt collar. Yanking him suddenly close, he peered into the man's watery blue eyes. "And I don't take kindly to them as threatens me. Maybe you ain't heard of Wolf Caulder before this!"

Short's eyes widened in sudden panic. He tried to pull back, his hands clawing frantically at Longarm's fist as it continued to hold him securely. Longarm heard Frida's chair scrape back as she jumped to her feet. He let Short go and turned to deal with the girl. She was reaching for that Colt she had stuck in her belt.

14

Longarm reached out and knocked her hand away from the weapon. Then he smiled. "Don't get nervous, Frida. I wouldn't hurt this old fart, not unless I had to—and I sure as hell wouldn't want to cut down a girl as pretty as you, neither."

The pink edge of her tongue moistened her upper lip. Longarm saw tiny beads of sweat standing out on her forehead. Longarm's smile did not waver. Cautiously, she sat back down at the table.

Short was angry, but suitably cowed. "All right. Five hundred. But you ain't got no call to treat me like this, Caulder. I'm only doin' my part, helping to get you killers on your way outa this country."

"Then do it." Longarm smiled coldly and leaned closer to the old man. "Now tell me. What's my next stop on this here Devil's Railroad?"

"That's for me to know and you to find out," the man said with dogged defiance, perspiration standing out on his forehead. "But you will," he added hastily. "Soon's I get my cut, that is."

"And who's this gent I'll have to dicker with?"

"You'll meet him at the next stop."

"What's his name, dammit?"

Short swallowed. "All I know is he's a big shot in the town you're goin' to. Owns the biggest saloon there, I hear. But that's all I know."

Longarm leaned back and studied Cal Short carefully. "And you'll be the one to take me there?"

"Not all the way. I'll get you out of this here county, sure enough—but as soon as you're clear, I'll just give you the town's name and the password."

"Password?"

"That's right." Short smiled, unable to conceal his pleasure. "It's a new one every month, and only I knows it. You pay me and I tell you what it is. Otherwise, you won't have any luck at all when you get to the next station."

"Very neat. I'm impressed."

"Thought you might be."

"Of course, I could beat the password out of you."

15

"Maybe you could and maybe you couldn't," Short said with sullen defiance. "But how would you know if I gave you the right word? It might not be the one for this month."

"And that would warn off that gent I'm supposed to meet, right?"

"Yessir," said Short, nodding his head emphatically. Then he chuckled coldly. "And it would maybe get you a heavy dose of lead poisoning, too."

"All right, then. When do we leave?"

"Tomorrow's soon enough for me."

"About what time?"

"First thing in the morning."

"That ain't very wise, is it? I expect these hills around here will be crawling with posses filled with outraged farmers and cattlemen. After all, that was their savin's I lifted this morning. I don't see why we're in such a hurry. We could wait until nightfall to move out, at least."

"Oh, them posses'll be out there, sure enough," admitted Short slyly. "But I got me a wagon hid away in the trees on the other side of the meadow. It's got a false bottom. You'll fit into it real snug whenever we come upon any posse or ride through any towns."

"I don't know if I like the sound of that. We might not always see a posse before it sees us."

"Suit yourself, Caulder," the man said with a shrug. "We can leave at night if you've a mind. But, hell, you forget. I've done all this before, and I ain't let a man get caught yet."

"That's a comfort, I guess." Longarm regarded Short coolly. "You say you ain't let a man get caught yet. About how many men might that be, would you say?"

Short's eyes lit thoughtfully as he calculated. "Since I started, maybe forty-one, all told. I think you'll make it forty-two, if I remember it right."

Longarm chucked his hat off his forehead and leaned casually back in his chair. "That's settled, then. We'll leave tomorrow night." He peered at the old man quizzically. "Don't that five hundred entitle me to any vittles? I'm as empty as a rainbarrel in midsummer."

It was Frida who got up. "I'll get him his supper," she told Short.

Short nodded at the girl, then leaned back in his chair, his eyes following her affectionately as she reached the stove and reached for the frying pan. He turned and winked at Longarm. Longarm nodded in agreement. Frida was some find, all right. The old man sure enough had good reason to be pleased, finding the likes of her this far from civilization.

Frida was a good cook. Longarm felt pleasantly sated as he fixed his bedroll under the stars, a good distance from Short's cabin, on a knoll overlooking the meadow. Short had not been at all unhappy when Longarm had announced his intention of sleeping away from the cabin; indeed, as Longarm had eaten, Short had somewhat clumsily intimated that he did not have very much room inside his small cabin.

As he took off his hat and placed it beside the saddle he was using for a pillow, he heard a light footfall in the darkness behind him. Pretending that he heard nothing, he slipped into the bedroll. As he did so, he reached in under the saddle and closed his hand around the butt of his Smith & Wesson.

The moon was bright enough for him to see the shadow that fell over him as whoever it was moved up behind him. The shadow grew still. It was the girl. Longarm could hear her soft breathing as she stood above him. Then her shadow shifted as she leaned close.

Instantly, Longarm flung himself about and brought up the revolver, shoving its muzzle up into Frida's startled face. With a barely audible cry of alarm, she stepped hastily back.

"That old reprobate sent you out here to get your money a little early, did he?" Longarm asked, flinging back the bedroll's flap and standing up. "If he did, I am afraid you're going to have to go back to the cabin empty-handed."

"He did not send me," she said. "He doesn't know I'm

here. He thinks I'm asleep upstairs in the cabin loft. Be quiet. Put down that gun. I didn't come out here to hurt you."

"Oh?" Longarm bent and tucked the gun back in under the saddle. Then he turned back to her. "Then what is it you had in mind?"

"I want you to take me with you."

"And just why should I do that? You're a fine cook, I got to admit. But you're baggage that would slow me down some, and that's a fact."

"Please! You must take me." She moved suddenly closer to him. "You won't be sorry, I promise you! Let me show you."

At once she flung her arms around his neck and pasted her lips hungrily against his. He tried to push her away, but she thrust herself hard against him, her lips opening and her tongue darting with wanton recklessness deep into his mouth. For a moment he found himself responding. Good sense prevailed, however, and he attempted to push her away from him. But as he stepped back, his feet got tangled in his bedroll. With disconcerting suddenness, he found himself slamming backward onto the ground, Frida's arms still clasped firmly about his neck, her tongue still probing his with feverish insistence.

With a determined effort, he finally managed to pull himself free of the girl's grasp. "Damn it, woman! You almost strangled me!"

"Is *that* all you can say!"

"I could say a whole hell of a lot more, but I wouldn't want your ears to curl. Now suppose you quit actin' like a dance hall whore and tell me why it's so all-fired important for you to go with me on this Devil's Railroad."

"I told you."

"I didn't believe it when you told me before, and I sure as hell don't believe it now."

"Why, what do you mean?"

Longarm sat up and smiled at her. "You just went at me the way you think a woman in a cathouse goes after a man. But that ain't how it's done, ma'am, I assure you."

18

"And you would know, would you?"

"I ain't had to pay for it in one hell of a long time, Frida—but I know them women, and you don't fit the bill. You didn't kill any customer in a cathouse, and even if you did, you sure as hell wouldn't shoot him where Short says you did."

Even in the dim moonlight, Longarm could see the sudden blush that darkened Frida's face. She hesitated, then nodded. "You're right, Mr. Caulder, I didn't do any such thing."

"But that was the story you told Short."

"Yes."

"Why?"

"It's my brother, Tim. I've got to find him, Mr. Caulder!"

"You mean he took this here Devil's Railroad to get out of the country? What was he running from, Frida? What did he do?"

"That's just it. He didn't do anything. He got into a fight in a saloon in Ridge Town. A deputy sheriff was killed. Tim was the only one they could find the next morning, so they tried him and found him guilty."

"You're sure he had nothing to do with the man's death?"

"Yes I am."

"Go on."

"But before they could transfer him to prison, Tim broke free of Sheriff Dinwiddee."

"Did you help him escape, Frida?"

She hesitated for only a moment. "Yes."

"How did Tim learn about this here escape route?"

"A cellmate told him."

"Where did you get the money to get him onto this here railroad?"

"I sold our farm."

"I see. So why doesn't he send for you? Why do you have to go through all this business with Short and me to join him?"

"But that's just it! He left more than a year ago. He promised me he would write as soon as he got to South America, and that as soon as he could, he would send for me. But in all that time I have not received a single letter from him. Don't you see? I just *have* to find out what happened to him."

Longarm considered a moment, plucking absently at his eyepatch. He had been looking forward to taking it off as soon as he bedded down, but Frida's sudden appearance had made that impossible.

He got to his feet and walked a few feet from his bedroll, then turned and looked back down at the girl. She was still crouched on the ground, watching him hopefully. He could see the shine in her eyes as the moonlight caught them in its glow. If he took her with him, that would make for complications; yet he found himself unwilling to leave her here with that wily old reprobate.

It was only a matter of time, Longarm was sure, before Short forgot that Frida was young enough to be his daughter. And if Frida didn't cooperate with Short when that moment came, there was no telling what the old man might do—or maybe there was. Longarm had seen the look in Short's eyes whenever they rested on Frida, and that look had very little paternal feeling in it. Short was an old man, but he was not dead yet—not entirely, that is. Frida was playing a dangerous game, and sooner or later she was going to have to take her lumps.

"All right," he told her cautiously. "I'll tell Short you're going with us tomorrow. I'll pay your way."

With a grateful cry, Frida flung herself up off the ground and hurled herself at Longarm. Her enthusiasm was such that he almost went down again, but this time he was ready for her. He remained on his feet and caught her up in his arms, carried her over to his bedroll, and dumped her unceremoniously down on it.

"Now you listen to me, young lady," he told her. "You already got my promise to take you, so you don't need to throw yourself at me like that anymore."

"But that's not why I—"

"And you don't have to thank me, neither. So why don't you just quit while you're ahead and get back to the cabin? I'm a weary man, and I need my sleep."

20

"In that case," she said, patting the bedroll beside her, "get down here beside me. I need my sleep too, but I need something else first—and I think maybe you do too."

He hunkered down beside her. "Now what do you mean by that, young lady?" he demanded.

In reply, she suddenly began to giggle. He frowned, then followed her gaze and realized for the first time that he had been stalking about in front of this young woman dressed only in his longjohns—and that their carelessly buttoned fly was revealing a condition that until that moment he had been trying to overlook.

He felt his face go suddenly crimson, but before he could remedy the situation, Frida thrust her hand in past the buttons of his drawers. What she found there proved the wisdom of her remarks, and Longarm decided it was hopeless to deny her any longer. He pushed her down beneath him and answered her kisses with a passion and an urgency of his own.

Laughing delightedly, she began peeling off her Levi's, and a moment later, in her eagerness to get rid of her shirt, she lost a few buttons. And then her hands were just as busy with his longjohns. Feverishly, she stripped Longarm, and soon their two naked bodies were entwined as Longarm's lips caressed her erect nipples, while his big hands swept lightly down along the silken length of her body.

Her hands were busy, as well, and pressing her nakedness against his, she uttered a tiny cry of delight as she felt how big he had grown. In a wondering cry of delight, she pushed him gently but swiftly off her, then swarmed up onto his chest and proceeded to mount him. Letting herself down upon his shaft with an almost savage downward thrust, she uttered a deep cry and flung her head back.

The enveloping warmth of her charged him with a delight that almost made him drunk. He felt the fire of her swarm up from his loins until he could taste it. She rocked back and forth, teasing him, sometimes pulling all the way out before ramming herself back down upon him, laughing silkily all the while. With a wanton, delightful calculation, she varied his torture by suddenly leaning forward, almost pull-

21

ing herself free of him, her magnificent breasts crushing their warmth onto his chest. Laughing also, he reached up, flung his arms around her, and pulled her lips down hard upon his. Her tongue began to thrust deep into his mouth— keeping time with his own wild, upward thrusts as he flung himself deep into her.

He was no longer holding back. He was thinking only of himself. Abruptly, she straightened once more and leaned far back, grinding herself hard down upon his erection, hanging onto his hips with both hands. As he felt himself building into a fierce, almost painful rush to his climax, she clung to his bucking torso, uttering tiny cries of delight.

"Oh, Wolf!" she moaned fiercely. "I'm getting there! Right now! Yes! Yes!"

She flung her head back still farther and let loose with an exultant, keening cry. At that moment, Longarm also climaxed, pulsing helplessly up into her as she rocked, groaning, back and forth upon his engorged shaft. But she was not done—and with each shuddering spasm she uttered a husky, delighted groan.

At last, whimpering, she collapsed forward onto him. He couldn't tell if she was laughing or crying as he covered her hot, sweat-streaked face with kisses. He gentled her, caressing her back with his big hands and speaking softly to her, as the wild pounding of her heart slowly quieted. Still on top of him, she moved luxuriously over his long torso, seeming to want to burrow deep inside of him. Her arms snaked happily about his neck.

"I just knew you'd be like that," she said, as she hugged him still closer. "I could tell. You're so big . . . and gentle. Like a dapple gray I had once.",

"What's that?" Longarm asked in mock dismay. "A horse? My you *are* talented."

"Silly! You know what I mean." To punish him, she caught one of his earlobes with her incisors and bit gently.

"Easy," he warned her, laughing.

As she let go, he turned his head to kiss her and caught sight of the shadowy figure that loomed suddenly over them. Without warning, he flung Frida off him and grabbed for his revolver, rolling away from her and out of the bedroll at the same time.

Short's double-barreled shotgun roared, and Longarm felt the fearsome wind of its charge as it narrowly missed his naked back. He kept rolling, then came up on one knee, the Smith & Wesson double-action pulsing in his hand. Short uttered a muffled cry and flung the shotgun up in the air as he was hurled to the ground.

Longarm had gotten off three shots, and it appeared to him that at least two of them had found Short high in the chest. As the man crumpled back into the darkness, Longarm scrambled to his feet, his revolver still in front of him, and approached the downed man. Short was still alive. The old man's body was slowly twisting. He was wearing only his longjohns, and in the pale moonlight he looked like an oversized worm that someone had just tromped on.

Longarm bent over the man, then froze. Short's right hand came off the ground. In it he held a Colt—its dark bore looking as big as the opening of a mine shaft. Longarm froze.

"Damn you!" Short rasped, furious. "You weren't satisfied with cutting down my share . . . you had to take my woman!"

"She wasn't your woman."

"Yes she was! Till you came along!"

"Cal!" Frida cried, rushing to the old man's side. "I never told you any such thing!"

He glanced at her, the hand holding the Colt beginning to waver. "No, you never did, but I was sure . . . hoping. And you let me hope, too!" His face went suddenly hard. "Damn you! You was too good for me . . . but not for this here no-account! Is that it?" He turned the gun so that it was pointing at her.

Longarm reached down swiftly and slapped the revolver out of the old man's trembling hand. As it spun off into the darkness, Short seemed to shrink visibly into the dark, bloody ground. Then Longarm saw clearly the two bullet holes in Short's chest. He heard Frida begin to sob.

The old man was still looking in Frida's direction when

23

he closed his eyes and sagged lifelessly onto the grass.

As Frida flung herself against Longarm's chest, he gazed bleakly down at the old man. Killing Short was something he would simply have to live with—but what added bitter disappointment to his dismay was the fact that now, after having planned so carefully and come so far, his route to the next station on the Devil's Railroad was locked forever within the skull of a dead man.

Chapter 3

A little after dawn the next morning, Longarm returned to Cal Short's cabin and closed the door behind him. The pungent odor of bacon and eggs filled the cabin. Longarm wondered how he could be this hungry after just burying the man he had been forced to gun down the night before. But there was no denying it; he was as famished as a wolf in midwinter. Frida was standing in front of the stove.

He said, "Well, that's done. You sure you want to go ahead with this?"

"Yes, Wolf. I told you last night. I've got to find my brother."

Longarm nodded and walked over to the table and slumped down into one of the chairs. Frida placed a huge platter of eggs, potatoes, and bacon in front of him.

"You'd better eat every morsel of this breakfast," she told him. "From what I've been able to find out, the next stop on the railroad is a long ways from here, close to the Canadian border." She planted a hefty mug of hot coffee down beside him.

He glanced up at her and smiled wryly. "Young lady, this here breakfast smells like you can cook almost as well as you can pleasure a man."

She frowned in some embarrassment. "Now that's enough of that," she said, smiling distractedly. "Just eat up."

Longarm did not require any more urging, and set to with a will. While he ate, Frida sat across from him and they went over once again what she had learned in the six months or so she had been living with Cal Short. Though she had heard other towns mentioned, the one town that seemed to her to be the most likely, since it had come up so often—and in this Longarm was in complete agreement with her—was a logging town on the Canadian border, Colville.

The contact there was a fellow named Sam Ogden.

Longarm decided, therefore, that the two of them would head for Colville and keep an eye out for this jasper Ogden. If they found him—and they should have no difficulty if Short's assertion that the man owned the biggest saloon in Colville was true—it should be a simple matter for Longarm to approach this "conductor" and ask for a seat on that railroad of his. If Ogden then asked for the password, Longarm had decided he would simply tell the man the truth—that he and Cal had fought over Frida.

"It's a long shot," Longarm said, lifting the mug of coffee to his lips. "And it sure as hell will be dangerous. You sure you still want to go with me, Frida?"

"After what happened last night, I don't see we got any choice," she told him. "There'll be posses still combing this country, and that wagon Short made works real nice, from the way he told it."

"All right, then. It's settled."

As Longarm finished his breakfast, Frida got up from the table and walked over to the door. Pulling it open, she glanced back at him. "I'm going for that wagon now. As soon as you can, fetch the horses in the meadow and follow after me."

Longarm nodded as Frida turned and left the cabin. Frida had already shown him where Short had hidden his wagon. It was tucked away in a grove of birches on the far side of the stream, bordering the meadow.

He finished Frida's coffee and stood up. He had to admit, he could not really blame Short for not wanting to share Frida with him. Among other things, she was one hell of a cook.

Leading Short's two horses, his roan trailing obediently behind, Longarm splashed across the stream toward the waiting Frida. She was standing by the wagon she had uncovered. Short had cut branches thick with foliage and hidden the wagon under them. As Longarm approached the wagon through the birches, Frida tipped her head and looked with some suspicion at him.

"You limped when you got off your horse and went into Cal's cabin yesterday," she told him. "But last night and this morning, I ain't seen a trace of that limp."

"I'll explain later," Longarm told her as he took the harness she handed him and proceeded to hitch up the horses.

She watched him carefully, then said softly, "You know, Wolf, I been thinking. A man as nice—and as gentle—as you was last night don't hardly seem to me to be the kind of gent who goes around robbin' banks and such."

"Now don't you go and let appearances fool you, Frida," Longarm said, slipping the bridle over the head of one of the horses.

"That's just what I'm saying," Frida said shrewdly, leaving him and starting across the shallow stream. "You ain't the man you appear, not by a damn sight."

Longarm did not know what to say. He just watched her go. When she reached the other side of the stream, she turned to face him. "Bring the wagon up to the cabin," she called back to him. "I'll have everything ready." She smiled. "Whoever you are."

Chuckling to himself, Longarm watched her move off across the meadow. There was no doubt about it now. He would have to tell her who he was and what he was about. It might change things between them when she learned he was a lawman, but he didn't see that he had any choice in the matter.

They had driven the wagon north through the mountains for close to an hour before Frida turned to Longarm and reminded him that he had still not told her who he was and why he was attempting to pass himself off as a notorious outlaw.

"You sure you really want to know?" he asked.

"I told you why I'm here. Now you tell me why you are."

They were following a stream, and Longarm decided this would be as good a time as any to water the horses. The team had been pulling steadily over very rough ground without pause, and he knew the horses needed the break.

As a matter of fact, Longarm could use one himself. He had kept the team close in under bluffs, following riverbeds and arroyos, being careful to avoid all high ground and ridges. As a result, they had not crossed the trail of any posses, nor been spotted by any, and for that Longarm was grateful. It meant he had not been forced to endure the torture of slipping in under the wagon's false bottom. He had examined it warily before they set out and had not been impressed. It appeared to have been built for a man considerably smaller than he was, and Longarm was convinced he would have had to twist himself into a pretzel in order to fit.

Turning the horses onto a grassy sward bordering the stream, Longarm hauled back on the reins, set the brake, and helped Frida down. As she untied his roan from the rear of the wagon, he unhitched the team and led the horses to the edge of the stream. As soon as the animals had drunk their fill and begun to crop the high, thin grass, Longarm and Frida both slaked their thirst in the swift water. Then Longarm sat down, his back to a tree, and watched Frida settle herself onto the grass beside him.

"Well?" she said, as soon as she was comfortable.

Longarm took out a cheroot, bit off the end, and lit it. "I'm a deputy U.S. marshal," he told her bluntly.

She pulled back from him slightly, making no attempt to hide her surprise—or her dismay.

"My name is Custis Long," he said, smiling to ease her fears. "My friends call me Longarm."

"Am I your friend?"

"I'd say that's up to you, Frida. We sure acted friendly last night, wouldn't you say?"

She blushed.

"Anyway, Frida, you shouldn't be all that surprised. Your brother sure wouldn't have been the only one to hear about this here Devil's Railroad. We've known about it for some time now. Quite a few hardcases we've been after have just up and disappeared, and each one that did was last seen heading in this direction. So the Washington office sent out one of their best men to trace this escape route and find out who was behind it. His body was found near Ridge Town, but in the dirt by his dead body he had written Cal Short's name. We did some checking after that, and it became pretty clear that Cal was the first station on this here railroad."

"Do you think Cal killed that deputy?"

"It could have been him. But we think it was someone else working with him—this fellow in Colville, more'n likely. Ogden. You ever laid eyes on the gent?"

"No I haven't," she said, hugging herself and shivering suddenly. "This is very dangerous, isn't it? I mean, we could get killed too, like that deputy."

"Yes we could."

She looked away from Longarm at the mountain stream, an anxious frown on her face. Then she looked back at Longarm.

"If you find my brother, will you bring him back?"

"If he is, like you say, a fugitive from justice, Frida, I'll have no choice. On the other hand, if he's in South America like he's supposed to be, I don't see that there's very much

I can do about that." He patted her hand. "So don't worry about it."

"That's not my worry, Longarm," she said. "I'm afraid he never *did* get to South America."

"Why do you say that?"

She shrugged unhappily. "I don't know for sure. Just the way Cal talked sometimes. It was nothing I could put my finger on, but I got the feeling that Cal wasn't being honest with them outlaws, that maybe they weren't really going where he said they were."

"That's something to think about, sure enough," he told her.

"I'm scared, Longarm," she said. "Real scared. There's no telling what could have happened to Tim. He might even be—"

He didn't let her finish. Pulling her close to him, he put his arm around her and began to stroke her hair gently. She clung to him, crying softly. He watched the horses cropping the grass and waited until she had cried for a while, then kissed away the tears that remained on her cheeks.

Three days later, Frida hauled back on the reins, halting the wagon on a ridge running alongside a swift-flowing river, on the other side of which sprawled the untidy little logging town of Colville.

Longarm got down from the seat. Swiftly wrapping the reins around the brake lever, Frida climbed down from the wagon also. Through a break in the trees, they were afforded an excellent view of the town and of the heavy wooden bridge spanning the river on whose banks the town was built. There were more than a few large, unpainted buildings along the main drag, along with the usual clutter of tents and tarpaper shacks crowding the narrow side streets and alleys.

There were two sawmills alongside the river, and beside them had been heaped great untidy piles of sawdust. As Longarm and Frida stood there, they could hear clearly the shriek of the mills' saws as they sliced through the logs, an unpleasant sound that shattered the primordial silence of this heavily wooded region.

Longarm nodded and said, "A place like this, tucked away up here along this river, would sure do nicely as the second station on this here railroad. I don't imagine the Canadian border is all that far away, either."

Frida nodded.

He looked at her. "You remember what we decided, now. I'll ride in on the roan well ahead of you. Give me at least an hour to get settled before you bring the wagon in. Just keep an eye out for me and try to get a room where I'm staying."

"All right."

Longarm saddled up the roan, tied his gear down securely behind the cantle, then mounted up.

Looking up at him, Frida smiled and tipped her head impishly. "Don't forget to pull that patch down," she told him. "It don't look like it's doing you much good, sitting way up there on your forehead."

Longarm smiled and pulled the patch down over his left eye. He had been wearing it up on his forehead ever since he had admitted to Frida who he was. He appreciated her reminding him of the patch, but he had not forgotten it, nor who he was supposed to be, when the time came for him to ride into Colville; it was just that he was not all that anxious to enter the place with one eye locked behind a damned eyepatch.

After he finished adjusting it, he nodded briskly to Frida, then urged his mount on down the trail toward the bridge spanning the river.

Colville had two hotels. One of them looked no better than a fleabag; the other one, recently constructed of fresh, un-painted pine, was situated on the town's main drag and was an impressive three-story affair, sporting a large veranda with deck chairs. There was a livery across from it. Longarm was cutting his roan toward the stable when he heard a sudden shout, followed by a string of magnificent oaths, coming from just behind him.

He pulled up hastily and looked around to see a pow-erfully built logger wearing a heavy mackinaw and stocking cap, driving a wagonload of logs down the center of the

31

deeply rutted street toward him. As the fellow cracked his long bullwhip over the backs of his straining horses, he let loose another colorful oath at Longarm and yelled at him to get the hell out of the way.

In no mood to argue, Longarm quickly pulled his horse around and waited for the wagon to lumber past, its great wheels creaking under the enormous load, the driver cursing with an inspired, almost religious fervor at the struggling haunches of his four powerful draft animals.

Continuing on to the livery, Longarm dismounted and led his horse into the barn. The hostler was a grizzled ex-logger, by the look of him, with a leather stump for a right hand and the side of his face scarred badly from a burn or cut, Longarm could not tell which. A logging accident, Longarm had no doubt. The fellow wanted two bits to look after the roan. Longarm tossed it to him, then crossed the street to the big hotel, not forgetting to limp all the way into the lobby.

He took a room on the second floor in the back, and gave himself a quick "whore's bath." He came back downstairs, found a chair on the veranda, took out a cheroot, and lit it. From his seat on the veranda, he was able to get a pretty good view of Colville. It was no more than he might have expected. As he had noted from the ridge, branching off from Colville's single main drag were a series of narrow, rutted lanes, sometimes no wider than a buggy seat, on both sides of which were ramshackle tarpaper shacks and tents thrown up hastily to house the various establishments whose purpose was to satisfy the loggers' appetites for sex, drink, and gambling.

On the main drag itself stood the solidly constructed—if unpainted—buildings housing somewhat more substantial businesses: the usual general stores, a blacksmith and a barbershop, eating places, and four very prosperous-looking saloons and gambling houses designed to attract the more respectable movers and shakers of this community.

Since it was midafternoon, the saloons were quiet. But a steady stream of rough-looking patrons still made their way into and out of the tents and shacks alongside the muddy

32

lanes, even at this hour. It would be more like a flood at the end of the day's work, Longarm had no doubt.

Turning his attention to what he considered the most prosperous of the town's saloons, a place called The Logger's Palace across the street from the hotel next to the livery, he wondered if this was for sure the one Cal Short had meant—the one supposedly owned by Sam Ogden. Short had said Ogden owned the best, and if this was so, there was every likelihood that Longarm would find Ogden on its premises.

As he thought this over, he found himself wondering about Frida. It was more than an hour since he had left her, and he wanted to get on with this business. It would be much simpler for Longarm if he could size up this Ogden fellow before the rush of patrons inundated his establishment later in the afternoon.

At last, as Longarm was reaching for his second cheroot, he caught a glimpse of Frida driving the wagon down the street, weaving it skillfully in and out among the heavier logging wagons that were now beginning to pour into town on their way to the sawmills. He did not change expression or pay her any undue attention as she passed within a few feet of him before turning into the livery. For her part, she gave no sign at all that she had even seen him.

Longarm was in the hotel lobby when Frida approached the front desk. He waited a decent interval, then followed her up the stairs. He had noted the room number the clerk had given her—number eighteen. He rapped softly. She opened the door almost immediately. He stepped in, took off his hat, and tossed it onto her bed.

"Now what?" Frida asked, closing the door behind him.

She was weary enough, but he could see clearly the excitement in her eyes. "I am going to visit The Logger's Palace before it gets too crowded," he told her. "The sooner I find this Ogden fellow, the better I'll feel. You stay up here and keep out of sight. This here town ain't a place for someone as pretty as you to be running around without an escort."

"I noticed," she said, smiling at him. "My, it's nice to

have someone who really cares what happens to me."

She moved close to him, put her arms around him, and rested her head wearily against his chest. He embraced her and looked down at her. Of course he cared what happened to her. How could he not care? And yet, this sure as hell was not the smartest way to conduct this dangerous an undercover operation.

If Billy Vail could see him now, he would more than likely have a shit fit and fall in it, Longarm thought, and he could not really blame him. Never before had Longarm allowed himself to take a woman along on a job. Still, Frida had been of some help, and if she was right and The Logger's Palace *was* the next stop on this Devil's Railroad, taking her along with him this far, at least, had some justification. But this far and no farther, of that he was now certain, no matter what the girl might say.

He reached down and cupped her chin in his big hand. "Yes, I care, Frida. So do as I say and stay out of sight until I find out if this Ogden fellow is in town, and if he's the one we want. You promise to do that?"

"I promise." She smiled wanly. "I need to wash up anyway. I feel so dirty."

He smiled at her, clapped his hat back on, and started from the room.

"Hey, Mr. Longarm."

He turned.

She held out her arms to him. "How about a kiss goodbye?"

He shrugged and returned to her. When he left her room a moment later, he was readjusting his eyepatch and trying to keep a pleased smile off his face.

The smile was no longer there when he limped into The Logger's Palace a few minutes later, purchased a bottle of Maryland rye from the bartender, and found a table in the back where he could keep an eye on the batwings and the bar as he drank.

The floor of the saloon was covered liberally with sawdust. The clean scent of it did much to soften the odor of

34

horse manure and unwashed men that hung in the air as well. The long bar extended along the left wall and looked to Longarm to be a Brunswick, probably fashioned of Circassian walnut. Behind the bar and running its full length was a fine, single-piece mirror; it was not only long, but high, reaching all the way to the ceiling. The Palace's four chandeliers were not too gaudy, but they were obviously quite expensive, each one sporting at least a dozen chimneys.

Longarm was impressed. Whoever owned The Logger's Palace was doing very well indeed.

Only a few tables were occupied, and these by barflies who seemed to be simply hanging on for the night's rush, when they might possibly be able to cadge a few drinks. A quiet, intent poker game was going on in the back. The pleasant click of poker chips floated to him across the sawdust. Filtering down from the upstairs, Longarm could hear also the occasional laughter of the saloon's sporting gals getting ready for the night's rush.

The few patrons bellying up to the bar had noticed Longarm the moment he came in and did not hesitate to stare quizzically at him as he poured a shot of rye into his glass and leaned back in his chair to sip it. Two box rustlers had been dozing at a table near the stairway. They had stirred themselves at Longarm's entrance, and now one of them shook off her evident weariness, got to her feet, and slouched over to Longarm's table.

"You all alone, mister?" she asked.

"Don't see no one else, do you?"

She shook her head wearily and slumped down into the seat beside him. Her reddish hair was cut short, and the rouge she had put on long before had streaked. The set to her mouth and the lines around her eyes told of too many men and too many drinks—and far too many empty mornings to think about both. "My name's Sal," she told him.

"Caulder," he said. "Wolf Caulder. Pleased to meet you, Sal."

She nodded absently, her eyes on the bottle.

"Join me in a drink?" he offered.

35

She brightened somewhat. "Don't mind if I do," she said, reaching for the bottle.

She lifted it to her mouth and took a hefty swallow, then set the bottle down again, her eyes watering slightly.

"I ain't seen you before," she said, wiping her mouth.

"That makes us even," he said.

With absolutely no enthusiasm, she asked, "You want to go upstairs?"

"Do you think you could make it?"

She smiled wanly. "Guess maybe I couldn't." Then she looked warily around her. "But don't tell the boss that."

"And who might that be?"

"Sam."

"Sam Ogden?"

"That's the one. You know him?"

"Do me a favor, Sal."

"Sure." She was eyeing the bottle.

He shoved it toward her. "Go tell Sam there's a friend here wants to see him—came a long ways, too. Just tell him my name. You remember it?"

She nodded as she pulled the bottle toward her. "Sure. Wolf Caulder. I remember." She lifted the bottle again, and took a much heftier swig this time.

"You better take that bottle away from her while you can, mister!" someone at the bar shouted. "She'll empty it afore you can say Jack Robinson!"

Laughter greeted that assertion, and Longarm took the bottle as gently as he could from the girl. "Go ahead, Sal," he told her. "You go find Sam Ogden for me, and I'll let you finish this bottle. And give you the price of another one to boot."

Blinking eagerly, she nodded in acceptance of his offer, pushed herself erect, and walked with a deliberate but surprisingly steady stride over to the stairwell.

Longarm watched her start up the stairs, then glanced at the bar. The fellow who had shouted was still looking at him, a shot glass in his hand. He was resplendent in a white shirt with a black string tie at his neck, an immaculate tan Stetson pushed casually back off his forehead. His suit and vest were a light fawn color and looked as if they had been recently pressed. The man was either a gambler or a drummer, Longarm concluded.

He was obviously hoping that Longarm would wave him over to his table, but a third party was the last thing Longarm wanted at this moment. He heard heavy footsteps on the stairs, turned, and saw a tall, rugged-looking fellow with jet-black hair, dressed in a checked shirt and gray trousers, coming toward him. Sal, staggering slightly by this time, descended the stairs behind him and followed after him to Longarm's table.

Longarm nodded a greeting to the fellow as he halted before his table.

"Sal tells me you're Wolf Caulder—and you came a long ways to see me."

Longarm nodded. "That's right. Would you be Sam Ogden?"

"That's me."

"Sit down. Join me in a drink."

"I'll join you, Caulder. But I never touch the stuff." He smiled suddenly, revealing handsome teeth. "I sell poison, I don't drink it."

Longarm shrugged. Ogden sat down. Sal hovered nervously in the background. She was waiting for that bottle Longarm had promised her, but she was obviously in an agony of uncertainty as to how to go about claiming her prize. Longarm was about to reach into his pocket to hand her the price of a bottle when Ogden, without turning to face her, snarled, "Get the hell out of here, Sal. Go somewhere and sleep it off. But be down here by nine or you'll be out in the streets before midnight. You get my meaning, Sal?"

Nodding quickly, her face turning deathly pale at his words, Sal turned and hurried on unsteady pins from the table. Stumbling awkwardly, she disappeared up the stairs.

"All right, mister," Ogden said, smiling coldly. "What have you got to sell?"

"It's what you're selling, and what I'm buying."

"I'm listening," Ogden said, watching Longarm closely.

37

"I'd like to go for a train ride. On the Devil's Railroad, that is."

Ogden looked quickly around, then straightened in his chair. "I'm afraid I don't know what in blazes you are talking about, Caulder."

"Sure you do. Cal Short told me to come here."

"That so? Well, then, where is he now?"

"Under sod, Ogden. Where I put him."

Ogden's eyes narrowed to slits as he leaned close. "Damn you, mister. You better be straight with me. Do you mean you killed Cal Short?"

"That's what I mean. I had no choice."

"Maybe you better explain that."

Longarm shrugged. "Short had this girl stayin' with him. She took a shine to me and he came after me with a shotgun. The son of a bitch nearly blew my ass off. Like I said, I *had* to kill him."

Ogden thought that over for a moment; then the tension in his frame eased somewhat. "Yeah," he said, nodding slowly and leaning back. "I heard about the girl. I could believe that, all right. The old coot was pretty taken with her, from what I heard." Ogden leaned back in his chair and regarded Longarm coolly. "And so Short told you about me, did he?"

"More or less."

"He gave you the password, did he?"

Longarm shook his head. "He told me there was one, but he never did get to tell me what it was."

"You took quite a chance coming here, Caulder—without that password, or Cal Short to introduce you."

"I took quite a chance robbing the First National Bank of Ridge Town, too."

"Yeah. I just got wind of that one. A nice clean job, from what I hear."

"Which means I got the money to get me a long ways from here, don't it?"

Ogden smiled. "If you get to ride on our train, you do."

"How much is the fare?"

"Half of your take is the usual rate—but since you killed

38

one of our most important conductors, the price has gone up. Three-quarters of what you realized from that job should get you well on your way."

"That's pretty damn steep."

"How badly do you want to get out of here, Caulder?"

"Bad enough. I've had U.S. deputies on my tail now for the last six months. The *federales* chased me out of Mexico. I think I'd better try South America. But I'm not giving you three-quarters of what I took from that bank."

"How much did you get, Caulder?"

"Ten thousand."

"I don't usually dicker."

"I don't have to go to South America, either, not your way. I could stay in Canada, maybe. Find me a nice place to settle down."

"Gets mighty cold up there, Caulder."

Longarm did not bother to respond.

"All right. Five thousand. Half of what you took from that bank. My cut will be twenty-five hundred. The rest will be due when you get to the next station. Do you have it with you?"

Longarm smiled at Ogden without replying.

Ogden understood. With a shrug, he said, "Hang on to it for now, then. We won't be leaving until tomorrow morning, anyway. You can give me my cut when you get to the next station."

"And where might that be?"

"I am not like that fool Short, Caulder. I'll tell you nothing you do not need to know. We'll cross the border tomorrow, and when we get to the next station on this line, you'll have my payment ready. Or else. Is that clear?"

Longarm nodded.

Ogden got to his feet. "You are staying at the hotel?"

"Yes."

Ogden beckoned to a man sitting at the bar alongside the dude who had spoken to Longarm earlier. He was a small, blocky fellow with a surly look on his pale face. Someone had long since bashed his nose in, turning it into a crooked button that gave his face a decidedly porcine cast.

As the fellow pulled up beside Ogden, the saloon owner said to Longarm, "This here is Dana. You'll be meeting the both of us tomorrow morning at six behind the Palace. You'll need a good horse and provisions for a long ride. Dana here will be your guide. And when you get to where you're going, he'll be taking my fee back with him."

Longarm nodded.

"And I wouldn't try to shortchange Dana, Caulder. He takes his job real serious."

Longarm nodded a greeting to Dana. Dana's nod was barely perceptible. The little man's eyes were like the twin muzzles of a shotgun. Neither man made any effort to shake hands. "I have the horse," Longarm told them. "And I can buy whatever provisions I'll need this afternoon."

"Good," said Ogden. "Until tomorrow morning, then."

Longarm watched Ogden leave his table and go back upstairs, while Dana returned to his spot at the bar. Longarm reached for his bottle. So far, so good. Ogden had not been difficult at all to deal with. The lack of a password had not fazed him, nor had what happened to Cal Short. It was, more than likely, the size of the fare they were going to be able to charge the man they thought was Wolf Caulder that made Ogden so willing to believe his story.

Or was it?

An uneasiness hovered in the back of Longarm's mind— a quiet but persistent voice suggesting that perhaps Ogden might have been a mite *too* easy to dicker with. In sudden exasperation, Longarm frowned at the direction his thoughts were taking. If he was going to start worrying like an old woman, he had better find a different line of work.

Longarm threw down the rest of his rye and quickly left the saloon, only remembering just in time to limp.

Chapter 4

Longarm got up in the darkness and began to dress. He heard the bedsprings squeak as Frida sat up to watch him. Pulling on his britches, he turned to see the pale outline of her slim body as she sat up boldly, her breasts glowing softly in the dim light, her pubic thatch as dark as midnight. The sight of her and the memory of the closeness they had just shared caused him to stir faintly to life once again, but he did his best to ignore it as he cursed his fly shut and reached for his leather vest.

"Do you really have to sleep in your own room tonight?" Frida asked.

"I told you," he said gently, slipping into the vest and strapping his gunbelt on, "it's just a hunch, but a strong one. You'll be safer away from me tonight."

"And from now on."

"I didn't say that." He reached for his hat.

"But you want me to stay here in Colville, not to go on with you."

"That's right. It'll be safer for you—and easier for me."

"But I've come so far. It's not fair."

He sat down beside her on the bed and put his arm around her bare shoulders. She rested her head against his chest. He had given her enough money to ensure that she would be all right waiting for him here for a decent interval. It was government money, of course, and Billy Vail and the other federal masterminds who had helped set this deal up would be furious if they knew how he was using this part of the money; but that didn't trouble Longarm. He didn't want anything to happen to the girl.

"We've gone over this already, Frida," he told her. "It's best for both of us."

"Yes, I reckon it is. But I don't like it, Longarm. Suppose something was to happen to you. I'd never see you again. You'd be gone. Like my brother."

"Then you'd go back to the nearest sheriff and get word to Billy Vail in Denver. I am counting on that."

Meekly, she nodded.

Longarm got back up and looked down at her. He could barely make out her features in the darkness, but he could see clearly the rich, dark spill of her hair as it swept down off her head and spilled over her breasts. "You going to be all right now?" he asked.

"Yes," she said.

Abruptly, she stood up and put her arms around his neck and kissed him on the lips, hard. Then, sitting back down on the bed, her hands folded in her lap, she said, "Now get out of here . . . before I start to bawl."

A few moments later, letting himself into his room as silently as possible, he turned the key in its lock, then took the room's single chair and set it down in the corner next to the window. Taking out his Smith & Wesson, he sat down in the chair and rested the weapon on his thigh, then leaned back so that the chair was resting snugly against the wall. Longarm was well back in the corner, his entire frame deep in shadow.

The dummy he had already constructed, before leaving

his room to visit Frida was lying undisturbed in his bed. It had been fashioned of pillows and Longarm's bedroll. After many years of this sort of thing, his mastery of such deception was good enough so that anyone poking his head in through the window would have very little doubt that he had caught Wolf Caulder asleep in his bed.

Longarm began to wait, listening idly to the loggers' boisterous shouts from the street below. He did not complain. The incessant racket was more than enough to keep him fully awake.

He was still waiting more than three hours later when—the loggers and the good-time gals having reluctantly abandoned the saloons and given up their carousing—he heard the scrape of a boot heel on the shingles of the veranda roof just outside his window. He straightened alertly in his chair and waited.

Longarm had left the window open slightly. He didn't want anyone to have to shoot his way into the room. Two hands gripped the underside of the window sash and slowly, carefully raised the window. A moment later, a head poked through, then a pair of shoulders. Longarm recognized him as the same well-dressed gent he had seen in The Logger's Palace, the dude who had suggested that Longarm take the bottle away from Sal. The man stepped through the open window and dropped lightly to the floor. Longarm caught the gleam of his nickel-plated Smith & Wesson in the dim moonlight that filtered in through the open window behind him.

Without a single glance back at the window—or at Longarm sitting in the corner—the fellow advanced on what he thought was Wolf Caulder's sleeping figure. A moment before he reached the bed, Longarm stood up, his own weapon trained on the man's back.

"Hold it right there, dude," Longarm said softly.

With a curse, the man swung around, falling swiftly to one knee as he did so. Longarm flung himself to one side as the sixgun in the dude's hand blazed, its thunderous report reverberating hellishly in the small room. Lying flat

43

on the floor, Longarm braced his right hand with his left and fired twice at the dim figure crouching before him in the darkness. Both rounds took the man, flinging him backward. The revolver in his hand detonated involuntarily, punching a hole in the ceiling.

As the dude's gun clattered to the floor beside him, Longarm got to his feet and approached the sprawled body carefully, aware of the sound of running feet in the hallway outside his door. A moment later someone tried the door, then began pounding on it.

Before Longarm could unlock it, it was kicked open and Longarm found himself staring into the bore of Sam Ogden's Colt.

"What the hell's going on here?" Ogden demanded.

"What's it to you, Ogden? You the town marshal?"

The man smiled thinly. "We don't need any town marshal in Colville, Caulder. And this here happens to be my hotel. Drop that weapon on the bed."

Longarm tossed his revolver onto his bed. "In that case, I am your guest. This dude here must have heard all about that money I was carrying, and came to see for himself. There ain't much doubt he entered my room to rob me— or worse."

Ogden looked beyond Longarm at the body sprawled on the floor by Longarm's bed. Even in the dim light, it was possible to see that the man's neck was a tangle of sinew and blood, while the lower part of his face had been almost completely blown away. Ogden frowned unhappily and looked back at Longarm.

"Hell! Sherm was my partner. You just killed my partner—after sending a message to him asking him to come meet you here in your room."

"Is that what I'm supposed to have done, Ogden?"

A few of the hotel's patrons were peeking past Ogden by this time, most of them in their nightgowns, all of them craning their necks to see the dead man lying on the floor beside Longarm. Ogden turned swiftly on the crowd.

"Get back to your rooms!" he snarled. "I'm handling this!"

At once the crowd retreated. In a moment the hallway behind Ogden was empty. Ogden stepped into the room and pushed the door shut behind him, keeping his Colt trained steadily on Longarm as he did so.

"You see, Caulder? I'm the law in this town. And you just broke it."

"I see. You don't really have any underground route out of this country. All you do is lure suckers like me up here, then take their money and kill them."

"Not so, mister. Only imposters like you. Who the hell are you, anyway? You ain't Wolf Caulder."

"You been chewing on locoweed? I told you who I am. I'm Wolf Caulder."

"You are like hell. I passed Wolf through here six months ago—before I set Cal Short up in the Bitterroots. That's how come he didn't tumble to who you were. Now who the hell are you, mister?"

Longarm shrugged. He felt suddenly ridiculous, like a clown caught outside in the sunshine after the circus left town. An odd thought occurred to him. Now he could take off this damn eyepatch.

As he slowly, carefully, removed his eyepatch, he said, "Name's Long—Custis Long."

The man swore softly.

Longarm was surprised. "You've heard of me?"

"You're the deputy Wolf was runnin' from—and quite a few others I helped through here, too." Ogden smiled, just a mite nervously. "Well, now, Deputy, it looks like you've done it this time for sure. Only on this railroad, there ain't no round trips. Not for you, there ain't. And your trip's ending right here in this room."

"You're going to shoot me down in cold blood, is that it?"

"You don't think I'm up to it?"

"No," Longarm said. "I don't think you are."

The handsome face was set coldly, ruthlessly. Longarm could almost feel the man pumping up his courage. He didn't wait. He leaped onto the bed, snatched up his gun as he hit it, and kept rolling. He was flying off the other side of the bed when Ogden's first round slammed into the wall behind him, less than an inch from his skull. The man *was* up to it, after all. Longarm was swtching his revolver from his left to his right hand when he heard someone enter the room and the sound of Ogden cursing violently.

Longarm poked his head up and saw Frida, both arms wrapped around Ogden from behind as she tried to prevent him from getting off another shot. She had been able to pin his gun hand momentarily, but as Longarm watched, Ogden flung the girl from him and raised his gun for a second shot at Longarm.

Longarm fired first. The slug stamped a neat hole in Ogden's shirt, just below his string tie. The moonlight flooding the room made the gleaming white shirt a perfect target. Ogden's eyes widened considerably as he stared with disbelief at Longarm, his gun still clutched in his hand. He started to raise it again. Longarm fired a second shot, catching Ogden in the right shoulder, and flinging his arm back. Spinning about from the force of the bullet's impact, Ogden sank to his knees and then toppled forward, coming to rest beside the dude.

Longarm got to his feet and rounded the bed. Frida, her hands over her face, was crouching on the floor. He reached down and helped her to her feet.

"Thanks, Frida," he told her. "You maybe saved my life. But come on. We're leaving here now. Ogden has another friend around here with very mean eyes."

"You mean leave Colville?"

"Yes."

"The two of us? Together?"

"Why not? That was a fine, brave thing you just did. And I sure don't mean to leave you alone here after this."

Longarm felt Frida squeeze him suddenly, gratefully, as he turned her about and led her from the charnel house that had been his room.

The sleeping hostler woke up fast when Longarm poked the man with his hogleg and suggested they trade the wagon Frida had left at the livery for a fresh mount and a saddle.

Longarm selected a solid-looking dun for Frida, and saddled it and his own roan, and well before sunup the two of them were on a heavily traveled, moonlit road that led from Colville north to the Canadian border.

As soon as it was full daylight, Longarm guided his mount off the road and directed it up a narrow trail leading to a pine-topped ridge that appeared to provide an unobstructed view of the road in both directions. Once on the ridge, he selected a grassy sward and dismounted.

"Get some sleep," Longarm told Frida as he helped her dismount.

"What about you?"

"I'm expecting traffic on this road—maybe a rider in a big hurry, someone anxious to tell the next stop on this railroad we're hunting that things have gone bad for Ogden, not to mention Cal Short."

Frida wearily brushed a heavy lock of hair off her forehead. "If we keep on doing this, we're never going to find that route my brother took."

"Doing what?"

"Killing everybody. First Cal Short, then those two in Colville. Do you always shoot to kill?"

"When another man's aiming at me, yes."

She shuddered.

"Get some sleep. You'll feel better after a little shut-eye."

"I hope so," she said, smiling wanly up at him.

Bemused, Longarm watched Frida untie his bedroll and go hunting for a shady spot. He would never understand the fickle sensibilities of women, he realized. They could be the cause of so much human damnation and slaughter—all the while crinkling their pretty little noses at what men had to do to save them from that slaughter.

He snaked his rifle from its boot, left the horses to graze, then found a spot on the lip of the ridge that gave him an unobstructed view of the road from Colville. With his back to a sapling, he settled down for a long wait—and soon his thoughts were picking their way back over the wild and trouble-filled events of the night before.

He was more than a little grateful that his nagging sense of something wrong had finally persuaded him to keep that tiresome vigil by his window. It had not dawned on him that Wolf Caulder might have planted that story of his being shot down in Mexico while he went north and took the Devil's Railroad out of the country—but what *had* occurred to Longarm was that all that money he was carrying would have made an excellent prize for Ogden if he decided not to share it with his associates in Canada.

It was just as well, Longarm mused, that he no longer had to go around faking a limp and wearing that damnable patch over his eye. From here on, he would simply have to decide on a plausible handle and an equally plausible history of murder and mayhem to go with it, and hope that it would be good enough to get him an introduction to the railroad's very clever—and very careful—ringleader.

The problem was, of course, that he was now once again in danger of being recognized by any of those hardcases who might know him and be serving as one of his "conductors."

He glanced down at the Smith & Wesson on his hip. It was a good enough weapon, and hours of practice had made him almost as good a shot with it as he was with his own Colt Model T. Even so, he sure as hell missed his old Colt resting comfortably in its cross-draw rig, just as he'd known he would. And while the Sharps was a fine rifle, with its flat trajectory and long range, he preferred the Winchester he'd left back in Denver; with it, he could fire fifteen rounds in the time it took him to get off three or four with the Sharps. But hell, he knew it wasn't a good idea for a man to get too attached to any one kind of weapon. A time might come when he'd find himself without his favorite little play-pretty, and then it might not matter how good he was with it. . . .

The clatter of hoofbeats broke into Longarm's gloomy thoughts.

Swiftly he lay himself down flat on the grass and thrust the Sharps out in front of him. Just as he had hoped, the rider was that pig-faced jasper who was supposed to have been Longarm's escort to the next stop—the one Ogden said took his work real seriously. The little man was lashing his mount like there was no tomorrow—and as if the poor critter had an elephant's hide. Longarm's mouth set firmly as he pushed himself up onto his left elbow, tucked the rifle's stock into his shoulder, tracked the rider, then squeezed off a shot.

The ground in front of the horse exploded. Longarm reloaded quickly, tracked a second time, and fired again. By then the rider had pulled his mount to a sliding, hock rattling halt. As Longarm's second shot smashed into the face of a boulder just behind Dana, he flung himself to the ground and began to snake along it toward a clump of alders. Longarm got quickly to his feet, reloaded and aimed very carefully, and put a shot just between Dana and the nearest tree.

As he opened the breech and thumbed in another cartridge, Longarm called down, "Stay right where you are, Dana—or I'll take off your hat with the next round!"

The little man froze.

"That's fine," said Longarm, as he slanted swiftly down the steep slope toward the prostrate man.

As Longarm came up behind him, Dana turned his head carefully and allowed himself to lift his head slightly off the ground. "You son of a bitch," he whispered hoarsely. Longarm saw the cold sweat still standing out on his face and chuckled coldly; the man had sand in his craw, all right. He would have to give him that much, at least.

"Where you going in such an all-fired hurry, Dana?" Longarm asked, as he bent and took the man's sixgun from his holster and stuck it into his belt. "Could it be the next station on this railroad you and Ogden been running?"

"Hell, no. I was just in a hurry, looking for a good place to take a leak."

"That so?"

"Yes, you bastard. That's so."

Longarm took out his revolver, aimed almost casually down at Dana, and fired. The round chewed up the ground a few inches from Dana's head, the explosion of soil momentarily blinding the man.

"Longarm!" Frida called as she scrambled down the steep

49

slope to his side. "My God! What are you doing?"

"Teaching him some manners," he said, as she pulled up beside him. "He has a fearful tongue." Glancing back at Dana, he said, "What about it, Dana? You going to tell me where you were going?"

"You killed Ogden and Sherm! And Cal Short. Who the hell are you, mister? What the hell are you after? You ain't Wolf Caulder, like you said. We knew that as soon as you walked into The Logger's Palace."

"That's right. I ain't Wolf Caulder. I'm a deputy U.S. marshal, and I'm not going to ask too many more times where you were heading. You fellows have already killed one of ours. I'm just doing my bit to even the score."

"Even the score? Hell, you're a mad dog!"

"Ever hear of the pot calling the kettle black?"

"You won't get away with this, deputy! That's a promise!"

Longarm fired down at Dana a second time. The round snicked through his hatbrim and narrowly missed his cheek.

"Longarm!" Frida cried.

"Stay out of this, Frida," Longarm told her with sudden, brutal curtness. She recoiled as if he had struck her. He looked back down at Dana. "Well?" he demanded.

"Damn you, Deputy. What do you want?"

"Where's the next stop on this here railroad? Who do I see and what's the password?"

Dana's dark eyes stared with unblinking ferocity up at Longarm. "And if I tell you?"

"I won't kill you."

"How do I know that?"

"You don't."

"The town is Albert. It's in Canada, a few hundred miles from the coast. In the mountains. There's a train there to take you to the coast."

"How long should it take us to get to Albert?"

"A week."

"You were driving that horse of yours pretty hard for a week-long ride."

"Before I cross the border, there's a small town where I can get more horseflesh."

"Who do I see in Albert?"

"Silas Wyman."

"And the password?"

Dana smiled wolfishly. "You don't need one."

"What *do* I need?"

"You need me to introduce you—and vouch for you."

Longarm sighed. "Then I guess you're elected."

"Damn you. You can't make me."

"Whether I can or not is what we'll find out, sure enough." Longarm stood back and waggled his gun. "Get up."

As Dana stood up, Longarm glanced swiftly over at Frida. "Search him," he told her. "Look for knives and small revolvers."

She nodded nervously and frisked Dana gently but thoroughly. Then she stepped quickly back. "Nothing," she said.

"All right," he told her. "Go back up onto the ridge and get the horses. From now on we've got ourselves a prisoner—and someone who just might take us to your brother."

She turned and hurried back up the slope. Dana watched her go, then glanced at Longarm.

"The two of you are sure as hell going to have your hands full. I'm going to warn you right now, Deputy. I'll get you first, then I'll take my time with her." His smile was chilling. "All the time I need."

Longarm stepped closer to Dana and punched him in the face. The man went spinning to the ground. On his hands and knees, his head hanging, his nose dripping blood, he shook his head to clear it, then looked back up at Longarm.

"You heard what I said, Deputy," he spat. "All the time I need."

In the hours that followed, Dana's quiet ferocity had a chilling effect on both Longarm and Frida. It also caused Longarm to treat the man with considerably more caution—and cruelty—than he ordinarily would have.

He forced Dana to ride with his right arm lashed securely behind his back and both legs tied together with a rope looped under the horse's belly. When they dismounted for

51

rest and food, and finally for the night's camp, Longarm trussed the man up as securely as a turkey on the way to market—tying both ankles and wrists, with the rope passing over Dana's shoulder, then looped around his neck, connecting the man's ankles to his wrists in such a way that any attempt he made to struggle or pull himself loose would simply increase the pressure on his neck. If the man got too ambitious, he could very well strangle himself.

It was difficult if not almost impossible, Longarm realized, for Dana to sleep, trussed up in this fashion, but Longarm paid no heed to the man's protests, and eventually Dana slept—much better, in fact, than did Longarm and Frida, who took turns watching their prisoner through the first night.

Early the next day they crossed into British Columbia, and after a few hours' ride they topped a rise that gave them a view—a couple of miles distant, in a heavily wooded valley—of the town Dana had indicated earlier was the place he had intended to change mounts. It was called Lone Pine, and was a small frame-and-log settlement with a single dusty, rutted main street and no railroad.

They dismounted, and Longarm untied the groggy, sullenly wrathful Dana and helped him out of his saddle. The man's legs had been tied so tightly that his feet were of little use to him. Longarm helped the man over to a tree and let him down none too gently.

"Thanks, you son of a bitch," Dana said, his coal-black eyes gleaming up at Longarm with a dreadful hatred.

"You're welcome."

"Loosen up my wrists and ankles, for Chrissake, or I'll lose them."

"You'll be all right."

Dana moistened dry lips. "I'm telling you, Deputy. You better kill me soon. Because if I ever get free of this rope, it won't be pretty what I do to you—and to that pretty little harlot of yours."

Swallowing the urge to flatten still further the little man's piggish nose, Longarm turned and left him. He was already angry with himself for having struck the man earlier.

52

Frida had dismounted and was slumped back against a tree. She had been watching the two of them wearily. "What did he say?" she asked.

"He said what a fine day it was, and he hopes we are enjoying our trip into Canada."

She looked at him in sudden exasperation. "Honestly, Longarm. We're both so tired, couldn't you just be serious with me?"

"I could, I reckon," said Longarm. "But I'm just as weary as you are, Frida. So why don't you hold off on some of your questions?"

His rebuke, gentle as he tried to make it, caused her face to darken with chagrin. "I'm sorry, Longarm," she said. "It's just that I've never had to do anything like this before."

"Like what?"

"Keep another human being a prisoner—all tied up that way, like a slave or a convict."

Longarm shrugged. "Just be sure you remember that he *is* our prisoner, and that it's pretty damn likely he had quite a bit to do with your brother's disappearance."

She sighed and ran her hand distractedly through her hair. "Yes, of course. You're right, Longarm."

He patted her comfortingly on the shoulder, then looked back down the slope at the town. "We can't take our prisoner into this town with us, not tied up like he is," Longarm said. "And I wouldn't want to untie him now—not in the state he's in. Right now I'd say he's as treacherous as a wildcat on a short leash."

Frida nodded

"So I'll ride in and pick up a packhorse and such provisions as we need. You stay here and keep an eye on Dana. I won't be long."

"All right."

Longarm was not too happy about leaving Frida alone with Dana, but he did not see that he had much choice in the matter. He comforted himself with the fact that, trussed up as he was, Dana could not possibly pose any threat to the girl. Still, as he swung into his saddle a moment later and turned his mount down the slope toward the town, he

53

could not still the apprehension he felt.

He turned in his saddle and waved to Frida.

Still slumped back wearily against the tree, she returned his wave.

And then she was out of sight, a thick stand of pine coming between them as he rode on down the slope toward Lone Pine.

Chapter 5

The moment Longarm vanished behind the pines, Frida shuddered involuntarily and looked over at Dana. He was looking at her also. She wondered if that was why she had felt that sudden, premonitory chill.

She pulled her plains hat firmly down onto her forehead and left the tree to check on the horses. They had found some good pasture, but she wondered if there could possibly be any water at this height. If not, perhaps she should see what she could find on lower ground. It would at least keep her occupied until Longarm returned—and she wouldn't have to feel Dana's mean eyes on her. Something about his look made her feel . . . unclean.

She was just starting down the slope when Dana shouted to her. She stopped and looked back at him.

"These here ropes are cutting off all my circulation," he called. "Least you could do is loosen them up some."

For a moment she considered the justice of that request;

but then, remembering Longarm's healthy fear of the man, she shook her head decisively. Not only did she think it unwise to loosen his bonds, but at that moment it occurred to her that, to be on the safe side, it might be a good idea if she checked the rope holding Dana to make sure he was still securely bound.

Dana let her inspect the rope without uttering a word. But as she tugged and examined each loop, he kept his piggish face inches from her face and his mean black eyes boring into hers, a mocking smile on his face all the while. It seemed as if this inspection of his bonds was just a joke to him, that he knew something important that she didn't. At last, satisfied he was securely trussed, she moved quickly away from him.

He chuckled at her obvious fear of him, and she felt the short hairs on the back of her neck rise up. She had a momentary, terrifying impression that he had an advantage on her—that in the next instant he would step casually out of his ropes like a magician and grab her. She shuddered.

Somewhat rattled, she told him unnecessarily, "I won't be long. I'm going to see if I can find some water for the horses."

"Take them with you. They'll find it for you. They can smell water before a human can." He smiled condescendingly at her. "Didn't you know that, Frida?"

She did not intend to reply, and was about to leave him, when he leaned forward quickly and said, "Frida, listen. You don't owe this deputy nothing. Forget him. Untie me and I'll help you find your brother. I heard what you told Long this morning. It's your brother you want, ain't it?"

"Yes," she said, moistening suddenly dry lips. "It is."

"His name is Tim."

"You know him?"

Dana smiled. "Tim Terrill?"

"Yes! That's him!"

"Sure, I know him. I recognized you right away. There's a lot of you in your brother. The same eyes, the cut of your chin. Sure, I remember Tim. Didn't I help him get through—like so many others? Me and Ogden, that is."

"Where is he?" she asked eagerly, forgetting for the moment her fear of him. "Is he all right?"

"Sure, Frida. He's fine."

"But where is he?"

"South America."

"But why hasn't he written me?"

"Untie me, Frida." He smiled up at her. "Loosen these here ropes and I'll tell you."

His smile, and the way he looked at her, caused her suddenly to shudder. He was lying to her. He might have helped Tim escape, but he knew nothing about Tim's whereabouts now. She stepped back, feeling like a bird that had almost been hypnotized by a cobra—and had only just barely managed to save itself.

"You're a liar," she cried, furious. "You can't help me find Tim."

His smile went mean. "That's right, Frida. I'm lying. But you can't blame me for trying, can you?"

Frida spun on her heel and hurried back across the rise. She was about to plunge down the slope a second time when she pulled up. She had better keep an eye on him, she realized. She could not possibly trust the man.

But an hour later, when she looked over at him, she saw that he had managed to curl up on the grass and was apparently fast asleep. The horses were restless, and so was she. She needed fresh water as much as the horses did. Besides, what Dana had said about them being able to smell water made sense. Both horses and cattle could smell water as soon as they got close enough; she had witnessed this herself on more than one occasion. Upset at herself for having delayed this long because of her fear of a man who was so securely bound that he himself had given up trying to get loose, she walked over to the horses, gathered up their reins, and led them down the slope.

A little more than an hour after that, on the rim of a meadow that had been invisible from the ridge, she found a swift-running brook, its water so icy it might have come direct from the Arctic. But not until they had reached the midpoint of the meadow, she reminded herself wryly, had the horses shown any sign that there was water in the vicinity.

She saw to the needs of the horses first, deciding not to bother unsaddling them, then sat down on the bank of the brook and tugged off her boots. Rolling up the cuffs of her jeans, she thrust her naked feet into the brook and rested them on a large stone that had been worn smooth by the swift water. The cold sent delicious shivers of delight up her legs and through her entire body. But after only a few minutes, she lifted her feet out. They were almost blue from the icy water. She wriggled her toes to get the circulation back in them. At last she got them tingling warmly and pulled her stockings back on.

By that time she felt so relaxed that she almost lay herself down on the cool grass and slept. The wind in the trees, the calling of the birds, the bright, dappled sunlight—all this lulled her, filled her with sleepy contentment. For a second or two she nearly forgot the grim, almost hopeless mission she was on. But the moment she let her thoughts flick back to Dana, she felt a tinge of guilt at the thought of him back there on the ridge, completely alone, trussed up so securely that he was barely able to move. She knew she should get back to him, but fought the idea. It was too frightening to be alone with a man as unpleasant as that.

Her dun was cropping the grass close beside her. Out of the corner of her eye, she saw it raise its head swiftly, its ears fluttering nervously, and turn suddenly around. At almost the same moment a chilling shadow fell over her. She flung her head around in time to see Dana's piggish, grinning face inches from her own—as he reached an arm around her neck and then forced his forearm up under her chin, crushing it cruelly against her throat.

She gasped and tried to call out, but only succeeded in uttering a tiny, despairing croak. The pain in her throat was so intense it brought tears to her eyes. Struggling desperately, her right hand closed about one of her boots. Heel first, she clubbed back at Dana's face. She heard him grunt and curse her viciously. She redoubled her beating at him.

With a sudden cry of pain, he released her. She jumped to her feet and saw him clutching at his right eye. Blood was pouring down his cheek. Without hesitation, she raced to her dun. The animal saw her coming and backed hastily away, thrusting its head up in alarm, its ears twitching. But she snatched at its reins before it could turn about, pulled the dun to her, and vaulted into the saddle.

By that time, Dana had overtaken her. He reached up and grabbed her left thigh, then caught her around the waist. She twisted away from him and dug her bare heels into the horse's flank. The dun bolted ahead. Dana fell away. She looked back and saw him on his feet, running for his own horse. Frida galloped about fifty yards farther, then hauled back on the reins and swiftly dismounted. With flying fingers, she untied her bedroll and flung it to the ground.

Dana was mounted up by this time and was riding full tilt toward her. She knelt by her blanket roll and shook it out. Her Colt landed, gleaming, on the thick grass. She snatched it up, thumbed back the hammer, and with both hands steadying it, she swung around and aimed at the oncoming rider.

Though she had owned this weapon since she had begun her search for Tim, she had not shot a gun in anger before— and certainly never at another human being. She froze. His face distorted with rage, Dana urged his horse to a full gallop as he bore down upon her. He intended to run her down! Horse and rider loomed with frightening suddenness. Lifting her aim slightly and falling away before the on-rushing horse, she fired. . . .

Longarm was leading a fully-loaded packhorse through a heavy stand of pine when he heard the gunshot. Cocking his head, he listened as the sharp report gave way to a series of echoes reverberating faintly through the pines.

Somewhere above him was the ridge where he had left Frida and their prisoner. But the gunshot had come from below him. Unlooping the reins of the packhorse from around his saddlehorn, he left the packhorse behind and rode recklessly back down through the pines. It had been a revolver he had heard, not a rifle—of that he was certain.

He broke out of a heavy stand of timber not long after, and saw, less than a half-mile below him, a narrow meadow, bounded on the north by willows and scrub oak. It was against this backdrop that he saw the two struggling figures. He heeled his mount furiously, snaked his rifle out of its scabbard, and sent a round into the heavens.

The crack of the rifle reached them a second later, and the two broke apart. Dana raised his hand. Longarm caught the gleam of a revolver, a moment before the man fired at him. He ducked low over his mount's neck and kept going. He saw Frida rush at Dana. Dana clubbed her swiftly, brutally, and she fell in a heap at his feet.

Longarm swore bitterly as he ejected a smoking cartridge case and reloaded. He could not risk a shot now—not with Frida so close to Dana. He pulled the horse around in a wide arc to come at Dana from a different angle. Dana broke back across the meadow, leaving Frida behind. Longarm pulled up swiftly, brought his rifle up, sighted, and squeezed off a shot. The round went high. Cursing the single-shot Sharps, he reloaded, sighted again, adjusted for the distance, and fired a second time. This time the round caught the fleeing man in the back, spun him around, and flung him facedown into the high grass.

Longarm spurred his horse across the meadow. As he approached the prostrate figure, he pulled up cautiously, pushed a fresh cartridge into his firing chamber, and leveled the rifle at a bloody patch of shirt.

"Get up, you son of a bitch," Longarm told him softly.

There was no response. Longarm nudged his mount still closer and spoke again to the apparently dead man.

"I said get up. You're just playin' possum, and I know it. You can lay there like that if you want, but I mean to finish you off right now with a round up your ass."

Dana rolled swiftly over and fired up at Longarm. The round caught Longarm's mount in the chest. The animal went down so suddenly that Longarm was pinned momentarily under its weight. As he struggled to pull his left leg out of the stirrup, Dana staggered toward him and brought up the big Colt that Longarm realized he must have taken from Frida.

Longarm snatched up the barrel of his rifle and swung the stock at Dana. It struck Dana's gun hand. The revolver fired, but the bullet went wild. By that time, Longarm had managed to pull himself free of the dead horse.

He flung himself at Dana. With a crushing blow to the left side of his face, Longarm rocked Dana back. An ungovernable fury had taken possession of Longarm. He swarmed over Dana, grabbed him by the shoulders, and kneed him viciously in the groin. He heard Dana's sudden, painful intake of breath. Gasping, Dana staggered back, pawing feebly at Longarm. Relentlessly, unwilling to give Dana any quarter, Longarm followed him, punishing him with a series of hammerlike blows to his midsection and head.

At last Dana stopped his futile pawing at Longarm and staggered back. His own rage expended, Longarm straightened up and held off. For a moment Dana swayed before Longarm, then went down like an empty grain sack.

Still panting from the exertion, Longarm stepped closer, bent over, and grabbed the man's shoulders. He shook him. Dana's head lolled slackly around and Longarm found himself looking down into the unblinking eyes of a dead man. Examining Dana further, Longarm saw the awesome hole in the man's side where his Sharps's slug had exited. Swearing softly, Longarm stood up and shook his head. It sure as hell had taken a lot to kill the son of a bitch.

And then he thought of Frida.

He turned and ran back across the meadow. Before he reached her, however, Frida sat up and began to stare dazedly about her. But the moment she saw him, her face brightened like a lamp in a dark room.

"You're all right, Longarm! He didn't kill you!"

He grinned down at her and pulled her to her feet. "He almost did. But almost don't count. You all right?"

"He fetched me a mean whack on the noggin," she replied, her hand resting on the spot. "But I guess I deserved it, Longarm. It was my fault he got loose."

"What happened?"

"I don't know for sure. I was down here watering the horses, and the next thing I knew, he was behind me." She swallowed painfully. "It's still sore! He almost strangled me, Longarm."

"He won't be strangling anyone now, Frida."

Her face went pale. "He's...he's dead?"

"That's right."

She looked at Longarm for a long moment. "I'm glad," she said softly. "I know I said some silly things before about you having to kill those men—but when Dana came after me like he did, all I wanted was for you to come back and kill him. I know that sounds awful, but I mean it. I tried to kill him myself, Longarm, but I couldn't."

"There ain't no need for you to talk any more about it. He's dead and gone to his reward—a fearful hot one, I'm thinking—and that's the end of it."

She shuddered slightly. "I guess you're right. I suppose we're lucky he didn't kill us both."

"We were lucky, all right. But my roan wasn't so lucky. He was a fine horse. I'm goin' to miss him some. Dana's mount ain't exactly what you'd call a fair trade. You got any idea how Dana got loose?"

"No," she said, shaking her head in puzzlement. "I don't."

"I left my packhorse back up in the pines. We'd better go up there and see what we can find out."

"But...what about his body?"

"Dana's you mean? Leave it for the buzzards. That's about the best use he's ever been put to, I reckon."

It took Longarm some hard work to unsaddle the dead roan and transfer his saddle and bedroll to Dana's mount. And while he worked, it didn't help his disposition any to see the big bluebottle flies that were already beginning to swarm over the open eyes and gaping mouth of the dead animal.

He felt a little better when he reached the pines with Frida and found the packhorse waiting patiently as it cropped the sparse grass poking up through the carpet of pine needles. When they reached the ridge a little later, they rode directly to the spot where Frida had left Dana on his side, supposedly asleep, and dismounted. Kicking aside the discarded rope, Longarm caught a glint of steel in the grass. Bending over, he picked up the bloodied section of a straight-edge razor.

"This is what he must have used to cut through the ropes," Longarm said. "He probably had it hid on him all the while."

"But I searched him."

"This is only half of a razor, small enough for you to have missed it. Hell, I would have too, I suspicion."

"But why didn't he try to escape sooner?"

"He had to wait until he was alone, so we wouldn't see him working on the rope. There was no way he could do it with us watching—not without us noticing what he was up to."

"Then it's my fault for leaving him alone like that."

"Forget it," Longarm told her. "It's all over now, and we have a long ways to go yet. Seems to me we'll make better time and enjoy the trip more without that no-account glarin' at us, wouldn't you say?"

"Yes," she agreed, smiling for the first time. "I guess you could say that."

"Good," he said emphatically, pleased that he had been able to get her to smile once more. "Now let's get ourselves together. Dana said Albert was a few hundred miles from the coast—a good week's ride. He wasn't lying. I did some asking around in Lone Pine. A week will just about get us there. And when we do, I'll have to figure some way to make the acquaintance of that jasper Dana mentioned."

"Silas Wyman?"

"That's the one."

"But without Dana, do you think he will deal with you?"

Longarm shrugged. "I don't see why not. Don't forget, I've got a passel of money in this here money belt. That should go a long ways to makin' him believe me. Or makin' him *want* to believe me, which is maybe the same thing."

"I hope you're right, Longarm."

He smiled. "So do I. Now let's get a move on. We can

63

make quite a few miles before sundown."

As the two rode back down through the pines, Longarm recalled his confident words of a few moments before, wishing he could have felt as sure of success as he had sounded. Still, he had come too far now to turn back.

A day less than a week later, close to sundown, Longarm left Frida outside of town and rode into Albert, intending to follow the same pattern they had established in Colville. As he turned on to the main street, he noted what appeared to be Albert's largest and most luxuriant watering hole. But that was not saying much.

Huddled under the looming foothills of the Pacific Range, the town was a sad, rain-drenched huddle of log cabins and unpainted frame buildings, tucked into the bend of the Fraser River. Its only pride appeared to be the bustling, well-constructed docks and the train station, and as Longarm rode on past the depot, he was amused to see how gaily it had been painted in gold and red trim, with its fancy shingled roof, and real glass in the multi-paned windows.

The railroad was a narrow-gauge, and when Longarm glanced up at the towering flanks of the mountains that stood between this town and the coast, he understood well enough the need for a gauge that narrow.

The town's single hotel was a two-story affair with a restaurant on the ground floor and a livery in back. Longarm dismounted outside the livery, led his horse into it, then trudged around to the hotel's front entrance. The aroma of home-cooked food wafted through the lobby as he signed the register.

He had already decided on an alias calculated to advertise a man on the run—John Smith.

The adenoidal kid behind the desk looked twice at the name, then nodded hastily and handed Longarm his room key. Half an hour later, Longarm watched from his window as Frida rode in. When the desk clerk had gone back downstairs after showing Frida to her room, Longarm left his own room and knocked quietly on her door.

"Longarm?"

"Yes, Frida."

She opened the door and stepped quickly back to let him in.

As he entered, he grinned down at her and said, "Did you smell that food when you came in downstairs?"

"Yes," she said, closing the door behind him. "It smelled a lot more tasty than that salt pork and beans we been living on."

"Go on down and fill your belly, Frida. Then come back up here and wait for me. I wouldn't go anywhere alone in this town tonight, if I were you."

Frida shivered. "I don't intend to, Longarm. What are you going to do?"

"I'm going to visit the local watering hole and make some inquiries."

"Be careful."

Longarm nodded solemnly. "I will be that, Frida. You just remember not to open this door to anyone but me. Looks like we're the only two new arrivals in town, so I don't reckon us comin' in the way we did fooled anyone alert enough to notice."

"All right."

Longarm clapped his hat back on and turned back to the door.

"Longarm . . . ?"

Longarm glanced back at Frida. "Yes?"

"Will you please be careful?"

He smiled at Frida. He knew she was remembering the last time he had left her alone—with a man who had almost killed her. "No need to worry about that," he assured her. "I'm as careful as a granny crossing a mud puddle."

Longarm was stepping up onto the boardwalk in front of the saloon when he held up to watch the toy train pull into Albert. Letting out two short, anxious shrieks, it huffed into the town's depot. Longarm could see the train clearly. Its tender was as gaudily painted as the depot, with red the predominant color. The locomotive itself had a fire-engine-red cowcatcher and a gleaming brass, funnel-shaped smoke-stack.

As the train ground to a halt, a gang of brawny, grim-faced men swarmed out of the saloon past Longarm and headed for the depot. After them, at a somewhat slower pace, came a cadre of heavily armed men. As Longarm watched, the gun-toters took positions outside the depot, facing the town, their backs to the depot. A moment later, high-sided ore carriers rumbled up from the docks and were driven up onto the station platform. Soon the gang that had left the saloon began unloading the boxcars that made up most of the train. What it was they were unloading, Longarm had no idea—but that it was enormously valuable, he had no doubt.

He climbed the porch steps and shouldered his way into the saloon. Only a few men had remained inside. Three of them were holding up the bar at the far end, two were sleeping it off in a corner, and a very large fellow in a fur coat was sitting at a table against the wall, his big hand folded around a glass of beer.

As soon as he caught sight of Longarm, he raised his beer in salute. Longarm made a quick decision, nodded in a friendly fashion to the fellow, and walked over to his table.

"Join me in a drink?" Longarm asked.

"Just as soon as I finish this," the fellow said cheerfully. As Longarm sat down, the man tipped up the glass and swallowed its contents in a few swift gulps.

A dark-haired saloon girl in a red ruffled skirt and blue bodice left her table and bounced over to them. The ample amount of white skin she left uncovered below her neck made it a red, white, and blue outfit. She made sure Longarm saw as much of her cleavage as decency permitted while she took his order, then turned about with such enthusiasm that he had no difficulty at all in glimpsing her black silk stockings.

"Ain't that 'un a pippin?" Longarm's companion remarked.

"She is that."

"My name's Chills, Red Chills."

Longarm glanced at the fellow's bald pate.

66

"It used to be red," the man chuckled. "Now it's just gone."

"My name's John Smith," Longarm replied, reaching out and shaking the old man's gnarled hand. The big fellow's grip was strong and uncompromising. "It's a pleasure to meet you, Red."

"Smith, is it?"

"Yes."

"Now that's a real odd name, that is."

Longarm shrugged without comment.

"I don't figure you want to talk all that much about your past, do you, mister? Well, that don't bother me none. I got the same problem."

The saloon girl brought their beer. Longarm paid her. "If there's anything you want, just let out a holler," she told them.

"I'll do that, Sue," said Red. "Later. Don't go 'way!"

"I won't," Sue said. "I promise."

"Yessir," said Red, shaking his head in admiration as he watched the girl return to her table. "She's a real pippin, all right. 'Course, I'm horse-tied but skirt-free. You can reason with a horse or flog it out of him. But you cain't do neither with a woman. They's nice things, real purty, and that's a fact—but they is better free than captured."

Longarm chuckled. He saw the man's point, all right. Red was dressed in a fragrant outfit that consisted of heavy boots, rough woolen pants and shirt, and a thick, matted bearskin vest. Through sizable rents in his woolen pants, Longarm glimpsed yellowed, sweat-stained longjohns. A rough red stubble covered his face, which was as weathered and furrowed as a rain-washed gulley. But his eyes were as clear and bright as those of a youngster in a cradle.

"You got any idea, Red, what's so all-fired valuable in that train just pulled in?"

"Sure. Gold. It goes on a steamer tomorrow—on its way to Vancouver." He smiled, revealing a few healthy teeth. "But I wouldn't get no ideas, mister, if I was you." He chuckled. "There's them that's tried, sure enough, but they all ended up in the bottom of that river—or worse."

"That wasn't why I asked."

"'Course not, Smith. I understand."

"You live in this town, Red?"

"Wouldn't be caught dead livin' in a town. I just come in for some vittles and possibles—and maybe a peek or two under a skirt. I hunt and trap some in these mountains. It's fierce cold up here in the winter, but they ain't noplace left for the likes of me down in the States. So here I be." He cocked his head and peered at Longarm. "You figurin' on moving up here to Albert, are you?"

"Just passin' through."

"I figured."

"I'm lookin' for the Devil's Railroad."

The man didn't blink. It seemed to be the most natural thing in the world for Longarm to mention such a railroad. "Hell, mister, you just saw one of its trains roll into town not five minutes ago. You'll have to stay here the night, though. It won't pull out for the coast again until tomorrow."

"What's that?" Longarm asked, doing his best to mask his astonishment. "You mean that train that just pulled in—*that's* the Devil's Railroad?"

"Why 'course I do, Smith. Everyone around here knows that. Fact is, it's the only railroad that'll take you over the mountains to the coast, if that's where you're aimin' to go."

"And that's what it's really called—the Devil's Railroad?"

"Why, sure."

"That's a pretty unusual name, wouldn't you say?"

"It's an unusual railroad, friend. The thinking is, only the devil hisself could've constructed a route that dangerous and got away with it. Look here at the picture on this wall behind you."

Longarm turned about in his seat and looked up at the wall. With his eyes now accustomed to the saloon's dimness, he was able to see clearly the mural that covered it— a mural showing a train winding its way like a brilliant serpent over the peaks and through the valleys of a precipitous mountain range.

And above this mural—painted in bold red letters—were the words, THE DEVIL'S RAILROAD.

Longarm looked back at Red. "Well, well," he said. "There really *is* such a railroad."

"Surprised to find it, are you?"

"You might say that."

"Anything or anyone else you're lookin' for, Smith?"

"Yes. A man called Silas Wyman."

Red beckoned to the saloon girl. She hurried over. Red smiled up at her. "This here gent's lookin' for Mr. Silas."

The girl glanced quickly at Longarm, then nodded and hurried back across the saloon to the bartender. She spoke to him swiftly. The fellow had been busy cleaning glasses. After a quick glance in Longarm's direction, he put down his towel and moved down the bar, lifted the gate, and disappeared through a doorway. Longarm looked back at Red.

Red smiled. "You've come to the right place, Smith, and that's a fact. You might say this is the gateway to freedom for them as wants to shake the dust of a dirty past."

"What about you?"

"I can hide as well in the mountains. Don't need to go on any train rides." He took a healthy swig of his beer.

The bartender came back out through the door. Behind him came a tall, wiry man wearing a spotless shirt and tie and narrow, Eastern-cut trousers. His pale face was lean, his cheeks almost hollow. He looked like a successful banker greeting a new client as he approached Longarm's table, a cautious but polite smile on his face.

"My name is Silas Wyman," he told Longarm. "You wanted to see me, sir?"

Longarm nodded. "I've come a long ways to do just that," he said.

Silas glanced over at Red. "Business, Red. You'll have to excuse us."

"That's all right," Red said cheerfully. There was a glint in the big man's eyes that troubled Longarm—as if these two had some huge joke they were sharing between them.

"Don't mind me."

Silas Wyman looked back at Longarm. "This way, Mr. . . . ?"

"Smith," Longarm said, getting to his feet.

"Ah, yes. You just checked in at the hotel, I understand."

"Yes." The two men shook hands.

"My office would be the best place for us to discuss our business. Would you follow me, please?"

"Sure."

Longarm followed the man across the saloon, aware as he went that more than one patron took the chance to shoot a furtive glance in his direction. It appeared that Silas Wyman's real business was no mystery to the habitues of his saloon.

Wyman waited by the door for Longarm to enter, then closed it softly behind them. Without a word, he walked across his office and around behind his desk. Sitting down, he opened a drawer, took out a revolver, and aimed it at Longarm.

"Unbuckle your gunbelt, Smith," Wyman said, thumb-cocking the weapon, the iron glint in his eyes warning Longarm that the man was quite capable of pulling the trigger.

"I don't see why this is necessary, Wyman," Longarm protested. "Dealing with a gun pointin' at me ain't exactly the way I like to do business."

"It doesn't matter what you like, Smith. We are not going to deal, as you put it."

Longarm allowed his gunbelt to drop to the floor. "Why not?"

"My name is not Silas Wyman, Smith. What it is, you don't need to know. But the fact that you asked for Silas Wyman tells me all I need to know about you. It's a code name, you see, and it tells me that you are a lawman, trying to crack this operation. A plant." He smiled coldly. "What did you do to Dana Crandall? Kill him?"

Longarm nodded. "Yes," he admitted wearily. "But I guess I didn't kill him soon enough."

The door opened behind Longarm. He could smell who

70

it was. Red. Too late, he started to turn as the big man brought a gunbarrel down on Longarm's head. A light exploded deep inside his skull and he felt himself plunging down through a great, yawning hole in the floor.

His last thought was of Frida. She had told him to be careful.

Chapter 6

When Longarm did not return to the hotel by midnight, Frida realized there was trouble. She stuck her Colt in her belt, stole down the hallway to Longarm's room, and rapped softly on the door. She did not expect any response, and did not get any.

Then she moved lightly back down the hallway to the rear stairs. Once outside, she hurried along the alley behind the hotel, crossed over to the one behind the saloon, found a spot in the shadows behind one of the outhouses, and waited—her heart pounding in her throat. The stench from the outhouses, together with the sour, stomach-roiling smell of vomit, sickened her. But she stayed in the shadows and waited, convinced that, sooner or later, the saloon would quiet down and she would be able to sneak in through the rear of the place and search out Longarm.

She had watched the saloon's entrance from her window all that night. She had seen Longarm enter, but she had not seen him leave. He was still in there, somewhere, of that she was certain.

The night quieted. She heard the shouts of men riding off down the street. For a while there was almost complete silence. Abruptly the saloon's back door opened and four of the saloon girls left; they trudged up the alley past Frida, turning eventually into the rear of a rooming house further down the alley. Inside the saloon, a lamp suddenly glowed to life in a room near the back door.

She straightened alertly. Perhaps this was where they were holding Longarm. But almost immediately the lamp was snuffed out, and a few moments later the back door opened, and Longarm—supported by two men on each side of him—made his way groggily down the steps. He was without his black, flat-crowned Stetson, and she could see a dark smudge of dried blood reaching down the side of his head and neck to his collar. His wrists were tied securely in front of him.

One of the men helping Longarm was a big fellow in a fur vest. He seemed to be in charge of the operation, and spoke sharply to the other one when he stumbled in the darkness. As Longarm was led out of the alley and across the street, Frida followed, careful to keep well back in the shadows.

She saw them take Longarm to the train depot, then darted across the dark street after them. Peeking around a corner of the building, she saw the big fellow roll aside the door leading into the baggage car, then boost Longarm roughly up into it. Then he climbed in after Longarm and dragged the still-groggy lawman out of sight.

With Longarm safely inside the baggage car, the other one approached the rear of an ore wagon that had been left on the platform and let down its rear gate. Two men jumped down from it and hurried across the platform and into the baggage car. The big one in the fur coat was waiting for them. As soon as they had hoisted themselves into the car, he closed the door.

The other one turned then, and walked into the depot.

A moment later a lamp was lit in one of the offices. Frida slipped away from the depot and, still keeping to the shadows, made her way to the livery stable.

It was dark inside the stable, the only sound that of the horses moving restlessly in their stalls, and the silken whisk of their tails as they swatted flies. She moved cautiously past the horses until her eyes became adjusted to the dimness.

She was looking for the hostler, a boy of eighteen or so who had taken her horse when she had ridden in earlier. She had felt at once his reaction to her and had instinctively encouraged his admiration by smiling and keeping close beside him as he led her horse into the stall. Then she had taken the time to encourage him to speak to her, after which they had a short conversation. It had done much for his morale, she could tell.

It had been shameless of her, of course, but she had wanted to make sure the boy would take good care of her horse. And besides, she could never resist letting someone know she appreciated it when they found her attractive—as she knew this boy had.

She stopped before the stall where he was sleeping. Leaning close, she called his name softly. "Jed . . . ?"

He was lying curled up on a bed of straw. So soundly was he sleeping, in fact, that she had to call his name a second time before he awakened. When he saw her bending over him, he sat up quickly and reached for the lantern hanging over his head on a nail.

"No, Jed," she told him. "Don't light it."

Then she sat down on a wooden box and leaned close to him. "Jed, do you own this livery?"

"Me? No, ma'am! I just work for Mr. Temple—the fellow that owns the saloon across the street. And the hotel."

"How would you like to make some money, Jed—enough to take you out of this town, and this job?"

"How much money you talkin' about, Miss Terrill?"

Frida paused to consider, then said, "Two hundred dollars now—and another two hundred later."

She could see the boy's eyes widen in amazement. Then they narrowed warily. "Why, I'd like that fine, Miss Terrill. But . . . but what do you want me to do for it?"

She leaned closer to Jed and began to tell him.

When the grade became so steep that his body started sliding along the floor of the baggage car, Longarm came suddenly awake, reached out, and tried to steady himself. But he couldn't. His wrists were under his body and tightly bound. Fortunately the train leveled off, and gravity's insistent tug on his body slacked off.

The clicking of steel wheels on steel rails came to him with sharp clarity. He lifted his head off the floor and opened his eyes. From a narrow, barred window high on the wall came a golden beam of light that shifted even as he watched it. Still, it was enough to light the interior of the baggage car. He rolled over, and with his legs pushed himself back against the wall. His head struck first and a lightning bolt of pain exploded deep inside his skull, causing him almost to groan aloud.

At last, resting his back carefully against the wall, he peered around at the car's interior. There was an ancient potbellied stove in the center, a table and chairs against one wall. There was not much baggage, hardly any at all, in fact. Red was sitting at the table playing cards with two men, a kerosene lamp glowing smokily on the table between them. The mountain man was well armed. There was a big Navy Colt on his hip and a hunting knife in a buckskin sheath attached to his gunbelt.

Red had watched Longarm push himself to a sitting position without comment. Now, a thin smile on his face, he asked, "Have a nice nap, did you, lawman?"

Longarm did not bother to reply as he glanced down the length of the car and noted the two other occupants—an adult Chinaman and what appeared to be his son, crouched in the far corner. The boy was huddled close to his father. Both were watching him impassively, only the boy's luminous almond-shaped eyes betraying his obvious fear. The boy could not have been more than five or six years old.

At first, Longarm thought that neither of them were bound until he peered closer and saw the gleam of shackles that held each one by the ankles.

Longarm did not understand this entirely, but thinking about it—and about how he was going to get out of this pretty kettle of fish he had fallen into—only caused his head to throb even more painfully.

He looked away from the two Chinese and back to Red and his card game. Red and his two companions were too busy studying their hands to notice him, so Longarm turned his attention to his bound wrists. But he saw no help there: a heavy length of rope had been wound so tightly around them and to such a thickness that Longarm was immediately discouraged from even attempting to get loose.

He felt for his money belt and was not at all surprised to find it gone. Silas Wyman—or whoever the hell he was—had already taken his cut, which meant Longarm was on the last lap of his trip out of the country.

Only his destination was not going to be South America.

He thought of Frida then—alone back there in that grim little town. He was glad that before he had left her to enter the town alone, he had given her half of the amount he had been lugging around in his money belt. If she used it wisely, she would be able to get back to civilization—and report to Billy Vail.

That much, at least, he could say he had accomplished.

The train began to climb another steep grade. At the same time, the car darkened perceptibly. He glanced up at the barred window. The rocky flank of a mountain had come between it and the sun. Longarm dug his heels into the wooden flooring to steady himself as the train crawled up the mountainside.

He took some pleasure in the disgust of the three men playing cards. Red had had to grab the lantern before it toppled over, and in the process had lost his hand. It must have been a good one, judging from the heat of his sudden, furious cursing.

Then Longarm concentrated on steadying himself as the train continued its relentless creep up the steep grade.

•   •   •

Looking out through the window at the nearby vertical walls of rock that dropped away from the train's roadbed, Frida felt her stomach go queasy once again. They were so high up and still climbing!

Twice before, she had looked out to see the train's funny little engine pulling its narrow line of cars over trestles that seemed no more substantial than spiderwebs, while far below them—so far down that it made her dizzy to look— she had been able to glimpse the foaming streams that cut their way through these towering walls of rock.

She looked away from the window and leaned back in her seat. There were only two other passengers in her car. They were sitting four rows in front of her, both in the same seat and facing away from her. One was obviously a drummer, and the other a woman who had lost no time at all in catching the drummer's eye.

Frida had witnessed the entire disgraceful exhibition. As soon as they had pulled out of Albert, the woman had made certain the drummer understood what she was and what she wanted. She had done this not only with her bold glance and inviting smile, but also through the shocking way she dressed, with skirts so high that a portion of her stockinged calf was easily visible, and with a bodice cut so low that she could easily have used her cleavage as an additional purse—a usage of which Frida was certain the woman took advantage. But it was in the way she wore her hair—combed out brazenly, her heavy auburn curls resting on the shoulders of her fur-lined cape—that had trumpeted to the drummer her membership in the oldest profession.

The two were sharing a bottle the drummer had produced a few moments after he joined her, and now they were conversing convivially, in a loud, boorish manner that Frida found quite offensive. As she listened to them, Frida took a faintly malicious pleasure in the knowledge that before long she was going to shake up considerably this boisterous couple in front of her.

At last the train leveled off. Immediately, Frida came

alive and glanced out the window once again. Was this the place? she wondered anxiously. According to Jed, the plateau would come into view after a steep climb. As she watched the rocky, uneven ground stroking by her window, her view was suddenly obliterated by a wall of rock that gave way with equal suddenness to a lush, flower-spangled meadowland that was dotted with scrub pine as far as the eye could see. A blue mist hung like a halo over the plateau—just as Jed had told her it would.

Yes! This was the place, she realized, her heart suddenly pounding.

She jumped to her feet. The adrenaline racing through her veins caused her face to flush and her hand to shake as she reached up for the emergency cord. She yanked on it as hard as she could. With a screech that threatened to puncture her eardrums, the train ground to a sudden, lurching halt, as its locked wheels were dragged along the rails. The drummer and the whore were sent hurtling from their seats, while Frida found herself spinning into the aisle.

She caught herself by grabbing one of the seats, then ran down the aisle and out through the coach's door onto the connecting platform. Through the window of the next door, she saw the conductor hurrying down the aisle toward her. She opened her jacket and lifted the Colt out of her belt.

The conductor yanked the door open, his pudgy face florid with anger. "Young lady," he demanded, "were you the one who—"

He stopped when he saw the revolver in Frida's hand. His face paled in sudden panic.

"Now . . . now see here, ma'am," he managed, "there's no need for you to go waving that cannon."

"I'm getting off here," she told him firmly. "You come with me. Now!"

The man swallowed and nodded quickly. "Anything you say, ma'am. Just don't get nervous with that finger of yours on the trigger."

"I won't. If you do what I say."

Swiftly the conductor lifted the trapdoor over the fold-up steps, then descended to the roadbed ahead of Frida, and turned and took her hand to help her down. Frida kept the muzzle of her revolver inches from the fellow's face as she descended. The poor man was ready to drop. Beads of perspiration stood out on his forehead.

"Now take me to the baggage car," Frida told him. "I want you to open it."

"Just as you say, ma'am," the conductor replied, as he turned and hurried ahead of her along the tracks.

There was no other conductor on this train, since it contained only two passenger coaches along with the freight cars. Frida caught sight of the engineer leaning out of the cab as Frida and the conductor approached. When he saw the gun in Frida's hand, he ducked back into the cab.

"Tell him I'll shoot you down if he tries to stop me," Frida hissed angrily.

"Sam!" the conductor cried. "Don't do nothing foolish! She'll shoot me down, sure enough! Just take it easy."

There was no response, but as she and the conductor passed the panting engine, the engineer did not reappear or make any effort to interfere.

They pulled up in front of the baggage car. The conductor banged on the door. "Open up!" he cried.

There was a muffled cry from within; it sounded like a question. The conductor looked nervously back at Frida. She cocked her revolver. At once the conductor turned back to the door and pounded on it a second time.

"Open up in there, Red! Hurry it up!"

Abruptly the door rolled back, revealing the fellow in the fur vest whom Frida had seen the night before. There was a gun in his hand. The conductor flung himself to one side. Reacting almost without conscious volition, Frida flung her gun up and fired. The gun's detonation sounded as terrifying as it had when she had fired on Dana—but this time she managed to hang on to the weapon and saw the big man in the doorway drop his weapon and reel back into the baggage car.

Astonished at her own effectiveness, she turned to the conductor and aimed her smoking weapon at him. "Get up in there," she told him. "And help me up after you."

The man made it up into the baggage car in a single, frantic scramble, then turned and yanked Frida up into the car. She almost lost her revolver, and for a tense moment she swayed uncertainly as she glanced swiftly about the darkened car and saw not only a very astonished Longarm sprawled on the floor in front of her, but two very dangerous-looking men at a table, watching her with mean, calculating eyes.

"Frida!" Longarm told her quickly. "Tell that conductor to get Red's knife and cut me loose!"

She turned swiftly on the conductor and thrust her revolver at him. "You heard what he said," she told the man. "Do it!"

The big man she had shot was doubled over on the floor, clutching at his left arm just above the elbow. Blood was pulsing out through his fingers. As the conductor approached him, he offered no resistance. The conductor lifted the hunting knife from Red's sheath and sliced through Longarm's ropes.

Longarm stood up and took the revolver from Frida's grasp. The instant he relieved her of the weapon, Frida felt the tension ease out of her. For an instant she felt almost giddy—so light-headed, in fact, that she was afraid she might collapse. She reached out and grabbed hold of the doorway.

Longarm was searching the two men at the table. He took two revolvers from them, stuck the weapons into his belt, and turned to her.

"Let's go, Frida!"

She turned and jumped down from the baggage car, Longarm following after.

Longarm had wondered what could possibly have stopped the train that suddenly, and had begun to theorize about the possibility of a landslide. Then, when he heard the conductor's shaken voice, followed by his frantic pounding on the door, he realized it was something else—something that was making him afraid for his life. A robbery, perhaps? Then he thought of Frida—and for a brief, fleeting instant,

81

he wondered if this emergency stop could possibly be her doing. After all, she had saved his bacon once before. But the moment the thought occurred to him, he dismissed it out of hand. And then Red slid the door back, and he saw Frida standing there with that huge Colt in her hand.

Now, as the two of them raced across the meadow away from the train, he still found it difficult to believe.

A shot rang out behind them—and then another. Longarm looked back and saw the engineer, still in the cab, a rifle in his hand. As Longarm watched, the man fired at them a third time.

Fortunately they were almost out of range by this time. "Keep going! Faster!" Longarm told Frida. "He might get lucky!"

In a moment they reached the rocks on the far side of the meadow, and ducked into them. Taking Frida by the hand, Longarm took the lead as they began to clamber down a steep, talus-littered slope.

"No!" cried Frida. "This isn't the way!"

Longarm pulled up. "What do you mean?"

"Jed's got the horses!"

"The horses?"

"Yes. But he told me he'd be waiting just below the line of trees on the southern edge of the plateau. He said I couldn't miss it—that there would be a river just below the trees. There's no river here."

"Just who in blazes is Jed?"

Frida told him.

As soon as she had finished, Longarm returned to the rocks, selected the largest one, and scaled it as high as he could go. He studied the plateau. He could see the line of trees Jed had told Frida to watch for, but they were on the far side of the tracks, behind the train.

Meanwhile, a party of four men—each one armed with a rifle—had left the train and was racing across the meadow toward the rocks. Looking closely, Longarm saw that Red was not among them.

He clambered back down the rocks to Frida. "I can see the trees well enough. But they're on the other side of the train. And if we wait here much longer, we're going to have visitors."

"What shall we do?"

Longarm thought a minute, then told her. "I'll be a decoy," he said. "I'll stay here in the rocks. You go on a ways down the slope. When you hear gunfire, work your way around to those trees and find this fellow Jed. Bring him and the horses as close as you can, but keep below the ridge, out of sight, and I'll work my way toward you."

She swallowed. "All right," she said.

He started to climb back to the rocks, then paused and turned to look at the girl. "Frida, no matter what happens from here on out, I want you to remember what I tell you now."

She blushed. "Yes, Longarm?"

"You are the bravest friend this here deputy ever had."

Longarm saw the sudden glow that leapt into her eyes. For a moment he wanted to hug her, but realized that now was not the time for that sort of thing. Turning away from her, he climbed softly up into the rocks to meet that small posse he had seen hurrying toward them.

Chapter 7

Longarm had three revolvers in all, and a quick examination of each showed that he had a total of fifteen rounds. But the four men racing toward him across the meadow were all toting rifles.

He climbed into a niche formed by two boulders. From it he was able to get a clear view of each man. The conductor and the engineer were in the lead. Those two poker players who had been in the baggage car were not showing the same enthusiasm, and were hanging back somewhat. It was obvious they had been pressed unwillingly into service.

Longarm waited no longer. A revolver in each hand, he let off a thunderous volley at the group. The four men dove to the ground. Longarm heard one of them shouting orders frantically to his companions. Half hidden in the tall grass, the four men unlimbered their rifles and returned Longarm's fire. It was obvious they had not yet spotted Longarm's position; their ragged, undisciplined fire sent rounds singing off rocks well to Longarm's right.

Longarm waited until the men's firing fell off, then peered over the lip of the rock and fired another salvo, once again using two revolvers. This time, as Longarm had hoped, he was spotted. Immediately, rounds began ricocheting among the rocks about him like deranged hornets. He left his niche and, making sure he kept out of sight, clambered swiftly down to the meadow. Dropping onto his belly, he started to crawl through the tall grass toward the gunmen.

Even after Longarm had put the rocks behind him, the four men still continued to fire wildly up at them. Using his elbows to pull himself along, each of his hands clutching a revolver, he made swift, steady progress. The exertion was not doing much for that crack on his skull, however. It felt as if a Chinese work gang were blasting a tunnel through the back of his skull. Blinking away the throbbing discomfort, he continued to snake his way toward the four men, and soon was able to see clearly their muzzle flashes through the grass.

He changed direction slightly, so as to bring himself around behind them. It took some time, and before Longarm was able to complete his encirclement, their barrage ended. He heard them talking. There was disagreement of some sort. Abruptly, one of the men—the engineer—stood up brazenly and waited for Longarm to fire at him from the rocks.

When there was no response, he turned to look at his comrades. "See that?" he cried. "The son of a bitch is gone!"

The three others got sheepishly to their feet, then started toward the rocks with the engineer.

Longarm stood up. He was less than ten feet behind them. "Hold it right there," he advised calmly.

One of the two poker players started to turn. Longarm fired. His aim was good enough to lift the fool's hat off. The man froze.

"Drop your rifles," Longarm told them.

They did as they were told.

"Now keep on walking toward those rocks."

They started walking.

Behind them, Longarm picked up the three rifles, smashed each one in turn by slamming its stock against a rock, then told the four men to halt. "Now turn around," he said, "and unbuckle your gunbelts."

Only Red's two poker-playing buddies were carrying sidearms. They did as Longarm directed.

"All right. Now the four of you can walk back to the train. And remember, I said *walk*. The first one that gets anxious will get a bullet up his ass. Now let's go!"

They walked past him toward the train. Longarm followed after them for a couple of yards and fired a shot over the head of the engineer when the man started to look back. Longarm took a few more steps, then halted. He watched them go for a moment longer, then turned and moved swiftly back into the rocks.

Not long afterwards, Frida was introducing Longarm to Jed. The young man had brought their horses, saddles, and a considerable amount of provisions. He had taken a fine chestnut from the stable for himself.

As Longarm mounted up, he glanced over at the young man. "I figure after this, you won't be very welcome in Albert. You want to join us?"

"I ain't never seen what's on the other side of this here wall of mountains," Jed admitted. "So maybe I'll join you. Could be I might take that sail to South America with you."

"Then come along," Longarm told him, urging his mount west toward the jutting peaks that still loomed between them and the coast.

The western terminus of the Devil's Railroad was, according to Jed, the port town of Squamish on the Strait of Georgia. Jed knew nothing of the place apart from that, so when they reached it six days later, they did not ride into the port until after dark. Riding past the train depot, which was only a short distance from the docks, they noticed that the railyards were almost empty of rolling stock. The train they had abandoned more than a week before had come and gone, and was now on its way back to Albert.

There was a profusion of hotels—all of them bad. The best one they found in a quiet section of the port. After they checked in, Longarm left Frida and went with young Jed to make the rounds of the town's profusion of saloons.

The port was crowded with sailors and loggers, an odd and seemingly very combustible combination. The first saloon they visited erupted before they could order a drink, and within a few minutes the place was a shambles. With Jed keeping close behind him and giving as good as he got, Longarm was forced to punch his way out of the saloon.

"Think maybe we ought to give it up for tonight?" Jed asked.

Longarm looked back at the roiling mass of men that continued to pour out of the saloon, most of them still engaged in combat. From within the saloon, the sound of breaking glass had become a steady crescendo. Longarm winced as he saw a huge bouncer go flying out the door, four angry loggers on his heels.

"I hate to give up so early, Jed. We've come a long ways, don't forget."

"So you want to try a few more saloons?"

"You can go back to the hotel if you've a mind."

"Not on your life," Jed said, grinning. "You might need me to help you punch your way out of the next saloon."

"Let's go, then."

Longarm had come to like Jed. He had run away from his home in St. Louis three years before, and was quite proud of the fact that he had been able to make his own way west without any help. The list of jobs he had taken to keep himself alive was a long one. The only job he had not yet had—and was hoping someday to try—was cattle punching, which was comical in a way, since it had been his desire to be a cowboy that had prompted him to run away in the first place.

Jed had light hair, fair, freckled skin, and frank blue eyes. His smile was bright and boyish—and revealed two missing teeth. Lanky, almost cadaverous in build, he was a foot shorter than Longarm. He wore a buckskin jacket that sorely needed mending, Levi's, and patched boots that were a size too large. His hat was a battered, floppy-brimmed affair that suited him perfectly. He wore it well back off his forehead.

The night was winding down. The next saloons they visited were relatively quiet. They sipped beer for a while in each one while Longarm discreetly inquired of barkeeps and various housemen whether there was anyone around who might be able to get them on a ship to South America. He was introducing himself this time as Tom Welland, an outlaw who was in truth a no-account horse thief that Longarm knew was constantly in trouble with the law. Longarm was taking a chance that Welland, like Wolf Caulder, might have come this way before him—but he did not see that he had much choice.

Only blank stares or elaborate shrugs greeted Longarm's inquiries, and he kept moving on. It was Jed who decided, finally, that they might have better luck and cover more ground if they split up. Longarm agreed, after telling Jed to meet him back at the hotel in an hour.

Jed nodded and moved off. Longarm watched him go, a little uneasy about sending a green kid out on this kind of an errand—until he remembered that Jed was no longer a green kid. From the moment he had set out on that personal odyssey of his from St. Louis, he had lost that designation.

It was a little after midnight—almost an hour later—when, moving across the mouth of an alley, Longarm heard his name called.

"Hey! Welland!"

Longarm pulled up. Two men were crouching in the shadows.

"You the one looking to make tracks out of here?" the nearest one inquired.

Longarm nodded. "That might be."

"Where you thinkin' of headin'?"

"South America."

"It'll cost you."

"I know that," Longarm replied.

"We can't deal here," the fellow said.

"Where, then?"

"What hotel you stayin' at?"

Longarm told him.

"Go back there, Welland. And wait. This won't take long."

Longarm nodded and moved off quickly heading back to the hotel.

Frida was worried, and said so.

"I know it's risky," Longarm repeated, "but that don't matter. Now you stay here with Jed and keep out of it. I'll meet these fellows in my room. I'll be well armed; as soon as they come in, they'll be covered. With all this artillery I've got, I feel pretty safe."

"If we hear any shooting, we'll come running," Jed told him.

"You just stay put," Longarm told Jed firmly. "Your responsibility is to stay here and look after Frida."

"I've been doing pretty well, looking after myself," Frida stated, her face flushing. "And after you too," she added.

Longarm grinned at her. "And well I know that, Frida. But please don't argue now. I can handle this myself. But if I need money, I'll call down here to Jed, and you give it to him. I don't want these two to see either of you."

"All right," she said, her voice softening.

Longarm left her room, moved down the hallway to his own room, and let himself in. He secreted one revolver under a pillow and placed another on the floor under the bed. Then he took Frida's big Colt, sat on a chair that gave him a clear shot at the windows and the door, extinguished the lamp, and waited.

The sounds coming from the street below became muted, the shouts less, the thunder of horsemen riding out of town gradually ceasing. At last, with the town sinking into a fitful night's sleep, there came the squeak of floorboards outside his room, followed by a gentle knock on his door.

"Who is it?" Longarm called out.

"You spoke to us downstairs—about that trip to South America."

"The door's open."

The door swung wide and two men entered. In the darkness, Longarm could not be sure it was the same men who had spoken to him in the alley. He thumb-cocked his revolver and leveled it at them.

"Close the door and stay right where you are," Longarm said.

"No need for the hardware," said the fellow closest to him. Longarm recognized the voice. It was the fellow from the alley, all right. His companion closed the door firmly but quietly behind him.

"How much is this going to cost me?" Longarm asked.

"How far you going? Brazil? Argentina?"

"Argentina."

"Two thousand. You got it?"

"I've got it. Is that all?"

"No. You pay each of us two hundred and fifty now. That's our cut. You won't see us again."

"I don't like that."

"You don't have to."

Longarm thought that over for a second or two, then nodded. "Done."

"That's fine," the man said, obviously relieved to be finished with the haggling. "I like a man who don't quibble."

"Who am I dealing with?"

The fellow chuckled. "You don't need to know that— just like I don't need to know where you got this money and what you're runnin' from."

"Guess that's so. When do you want the money?"

"Just before you leave."

"When'll that be?"

"Three this morning be too soon? We got a ship standing off the coast right now. There's room on it for one more passenger."

"I'll be ready."

"Dock number three, Welland. It's the one with the fishnets hanging off the dock. You can't miss it. There'll be a dinghy waiting for you under the docks. The password is 'devil.'"

"I got it."

"You'll pay for your passage when you get on the ship. To the first mate, Bill Robinson."

"Bill Robinson."

"That's it. Now, our cut."

"Go on over to that corner there and turn your back to me."

"You don't need to do that."

"Yes I do. And remember, I've got you both covered."

Resentfully the two men walked over to the corner and turned their backs to Longarm. Longarm went to the door, still covering the two, opened it, and called in a loud whisper to Jed.

Jed appeared in Frida's doorway.

"Bring five hundred dollars."

Even in the dim light of the hallway, Longarm could see Jed's eyebrows go up. Then he disappeared back into Frida's room, to come out a few moments later and hurry down the hall with the money. Longarm took it from him without letting Jed inside, then motioned to him to get back to Frida's room.

Closing the door, Longarm told the two men they could turn back around. When they did, he holstered his weapon, counted out the sum in fifty-dollar bills, and handed each his cut. The men were immediately mollified.

As they filed out of his room, the one who had done all the talking turned and said, "Don't be late. Three o'clock, we said. That boat has to sail on the next tide."

"I'll be there."

The fellow continued on out the door, pulling the door shut behind him.

Longarm waited until they had started down the stairs before he left his room and hurried down the hallway to knock on Frida's door. Jed pulled it open.

"Follow those two men, Jed. They're leaving the hotel now. There's a good chance they won't know who you are, but stay in the shadows if you can. I want to know where they are going, and who it is they're taking their orders from."

As Jed hurried out, Longarm turned to Frida.

"No matter what Jed turns up, I'm going on that boat ride, Frida—and you and Jed are staying behind. You'll be safe with Jed, and there's a better chance the two of you can get back to Billy Vail if something happens to me."

"Longarm, take me with you! I want to go with you! If Tim's still in Argentina, I have to find him."

"Frida," Longarm said carefully. "I've been thinking about Tim, and I've been meaning to talk to you about him."

Suddenly wary, she said, "Why, whatever do you mean, Longarm?"

"I suspicion that your brother and maybe a lot of others have got no closer to Argentina than this here coast. This Devil's Railroad is taking outlaws out of the country, all right. But there's no guarantee it's taking them to South America. Where it *is* taking them is what I need to find out."

"But I want to find that out, too!"

"No. It's too dangerous, Frida—and I need you to get back to Billy Vail. You've got to tell him what Jed finds and what I think. He can get ahold of Canadian authorities, and get some kind of a net over this operation."

She saw that his mind was made up. For a moment, he could see, she was debating within herself whether or not to insist. Then he saw her resolve soften. She shrugged in resignation. "All right, then, Longarm. I'll do as you say."

"That's fine, Frida."

"You'll be going soon, then."

"As soon as Jed gets back. Supposedly, that ship has got to sail on the next tide."

She stepped close and flung her arms around his neck. Pulling his face down to hers, she kissed him on the lips. Then she pulled back and said, "We've got time, haven't we?"

"For what?" he asked, knowing it was a foolish question.

"For me to say goodbye to you," she replied, taking his hand and leading him over to her bed.

She felt his uncertainty and swiftly pulled the tail of his

shirt out from under his belt and ran her palm up his bare chest. Her hand awakened in him the hunger he had kept down during their long trek, with Jed hanging close as a third party. He bent and kissed her, then lifted her easily in his arms and placed her gently on her bed. He was on the bed beside her in a moment, ignoring the warning bells that sounded deep within him—and the knowledge that this time he had not secreted any weapon nearby just in case—as had always been his custom in the past.

Her lips swept away such concerns. She had been wearing only a long nightshirt, and was soon naked beside him. Swiftly he peeled his britches off his body, his lips fastened to her nipples all the while. His lips moved down her silken body until they found her belly. She ran her hands distractedly through his hair, then closed them about his thick locks and pulled him back up to her, her legs thrusting wide as she did so.

He rolled onto her and thrust forward, and found himself within her almost before he knew it, her slick warmth enclosing his erection with the tenacity of a fist. She pulled his face down to hers and kissed him, her tongue probing with delicious abandon deep into his mouth. As his thrusts became deeper and more savage, she thrust her thighs up with a sudden, angry urgency. Her lips left his, and to his surprise, she fastened her teeth about his left earlobe. But he paid no heed.

Her teeth released his earlobe and she cried out, then thrust herself still higher, wrapping her legs about his waist. He plunged still more deeply into her and heard a sudden, answering gasp of pleasure. She began flinging her head from side to side, her eyes shut tightly as she rose to her climax.

With a final, wild plunge, Longarm thrust home, impaling Frida beneath him.

"Oh, Longarm!" she cried. "Yes! Yes!"

Shuddering, Longarm said his goodbye to Frida . . . and she responded in kind. . . .

• • •

Not long afterwards, Longarm heard a soft rap on his door. Pulling Frida's Colt from his belt, he approached the door warily. "That you, Jed?"

"Yes."

Longarm pulled the door open. Jed stepped in hurriedly, his face betraying his excitement.

"What did you find?"

"Them two jaspers went to a warehouse near the docks. I followed them inside and saw them go upstairs to a second-floor office. There was a light on. They knocked and somebody let 'em in. I couldn't tell much from where I was, so I waited until they were through." He frowned. "That was all right, wasn't it?"

"You didn't get seen, did you?"

"No. I mean, I don't think so."

"Then you did right. Now what can you tell me?"

"Well, after those two left with another fellow—and that wasn't long—I went up to the office and let myself in. I didn't find much because I didn't dare put a light on. But I know who the fellow is they went to see, and what his name is."

"Let's have it."

"Sir Allen Pembroke."

Longarm frowned. "What's a man with a title like that doing here? Could you find that out?"

"He's an importer, at least that's what it says on the door: 'Sir Allen Pembroke, Imports and Exports.'"

"Did you see this fellow?"

"I'm pretty sure he's the one I saw leaving with those two men you sent me to follow."

Longarm considered what Jed had told him. It didn't help him much—not with his present problem, anyway, which was to stay alive once he found himself on this ship heading south. But at least now Longarm had a name to send to Billy Vail if anything were to happen to him. Satisfied that Jed had done all he could, Longarm told him that he was to stay at the hotel with Frida for at least a week, that if Longarm didn't get word to them by that time, he was to make sure that Frida got safely back to the States and that someone reached Billy Vail to tell him what they had found out so far about the Devil's Railroad.

With some reluctance, Jed agreed.

"Goodbye, then," Longarm said. "It's close to three, and I've a boat ride to take."

Longarm shook Jed's hand and let himself out of his room.

The dock was as damp and as dark as the inside of a snake's belly. Longarm shivered. The night wind was sending a cold breeze toward him from across the strait's waters.

He reached the end of the dock and looked out at the dark outline of a schooner riding at anchor perhaps two hundred yards out. There was a steady green light glowing on its bow. He waited, keeping an eye out for any small boats heading toward the dock from the schooner. He saw only empty water. He looked back at the shoreline. A jumble of dark buildings met his gaze. No one was moving up onto the dock behind him. Then he heard the unmistakable sound of an oar slicing into the water. It came from under his feet, directly beneath the floor of the dock.

"You got something to tell me, mister?" a voice called to him from the waters to his left.

Longarm glanced over and saw a dinghy slip into view from under the dock. The one who spoke was standing up in the bow, facing him. He was wearing a black pea jacket and a short-billed officer's cap. There were two other sailors in the boat, their backs to Longarm. As Longarm watched, one of them shipped his oars and turned to look at him.

"Devil," Longarm said.

"Right you be, mate. Climb aboard. Just be careful you don't take an early bath."

The sailor who was still rowing guided the dinghy closer. Longarm set himself carefully, then stepped down into the boat. It tipped queasily under his weight. He sat down quickly on a wooden cross-member. The fellow who had been standing in the boat sat down alongside him.

"I guess you'd be Welland," the man said, as the two rowers began pulling toward the schooner's dark outline.

"And you'd be First Mate Robinson."

"That's it, matey."

A boarding ladder had been let down from the schooner's deck. The first mate held it steady for him while Longarm stepped out of the dinghy and clambered up the ladder. He hopped over the rail and onto the deck. As the mate clambered up behind him, a bulky figure emerged from the shadows across the deck and walked toward him.

Red Chills.

The big man was smiling. He had not gone back to Albert on the train, after all. Too late, Longarm went for the Colt in his belt. From behind him, the first mate stuck something hard and unyielding into his back.

"You owe me some money, Welland," Robinson reminded him. "I don't want you to get ventilated until I see it."

Red pulled up in front of Longarm. "I heard your name is Welland now, lawman," he said, smiling coldly. His left arm was in a sling. "You sure ain't very bright. If you'd of stayed on that train, you'd of got on board a lot sooner and a lot easier."

Longarm heard a muffled cry from the water below. He glanced over the side. Another dinghy was approaching the boarding ladder, and its two passengers were struggling with a tall fellow in a lumberman's jacket. Longarm recognized at once Jed's floppy-brimmed hat and the bright sheen of Frida's auburn curls. As Longarm watched, one of the sailors reached up and clubbed Jed. Frida screamed a second time, but a well-aimed slap silenced her.

Longarm looked back at Red Chills.

The man was not smiling now. He said, "You did good, makin' it this far, lawman. But this time for sure we'll take you all the way, less'n you think you can walk on water. And when you get to where you're goin', you'll find it's one hell of a long way from Argentina!"

Only then did Red laugh.

Chapter 8

Longarm and Frida, fully conscious, were flung unceremoniously into a damp hold, the still-unconscious Jed following soon after. In the clammy darkness, Longarm examined Jed as well as he could. From what he could make out, Jed was suffering from, at worst, a nasty bump on the head and a sorely abused nose.

As the ship got under way, Frida sat with her knees drawn up under her chin, shivering from the cold and the terror, still fresh in her mind, of her brutal abduction. Longarm covered her with his vest and comforted her as best he could until at last she calmed down enough to tell him how she and Jed had been apprehended.

"As soon as you left," she said, "there was a knock on my door. I thought it was you come back, but when I opened it, that big fellow was standing there in the hallway—the one they call Red—and two others. Poor Jed. When he went for a gun, they landed on him something fierce." She shuddered. "He just didn't have any chance at all, Longarm. They must have been waiting right outside the hotel for you to leave."

"Cat and mouse," Longarm agreed. "That's the game they were playing since we got here, looks like."

She sighed miserably and leaned her head against his shoulder. "I guess that goodbye of ours wasn't goodbye after all, was it, Longarm?"

He patted her hand comfortingly. "No it wasn't, Frida. But don't worry. We'll get out of this in one piece. And maybe you're going to find that brother of yours, after all."

"Do you really think so?"

"They haven't killed us, Frida. And God knows, they've sure as hell had the opportunity. They're taking us somewhere. It won't be Argentina, that's for sure. But wherever they *are* taking us, they likely need us for something."

"But what?"

"I have an idea. But it's so crazy, I'd like to think on it a while longer."

Jed groaned and stirred. As Longarm left Frida and moved to his side, the young man pushed himself erect, his hand to his head. Longarm had a pretty good idea how Jed felt. There were times when his head still throbbed painfully from that clubbing Chills had given him in Albert.

"How do you feel?" Longarm asked.

"Like a herd of buffalo just trampled over me."

"If they had, you wouldn't be sitting up now," Longarm chuckled.

The deck sank under them and then rose, only to roll sickeningly to starboard as the schooner, fully under way now, plowed through the Strait of Georgia's choppy waters.

"My God, Longarm!" Jed said, groaning. "Where are we off to now? Argentina?"

"Not on your life. Somewhere a lot closer, I suspicion. This here schooner ain't big enough or seaworthy enough to do much open-ocean sailing."

The deck under them sank with sudden, sickening haste. Jed groaned. "I'm going to get sick, Longarm."

"You do, and I'll make you eat it."

Jed's eyes rolled up into his skull, but he clapped his hand over his mouth. Longarm moved back to Frida:

"Would you really?" she asked. "I mean, make poor Jed—"

"I would. This ain't going to be a holiday as it is."

"Even," she asked in a small voice, "if it were me?"

"Yes."

She hugged her knees closer to her. "All right," she said grimly, her voice small. "I'll remember that."

The door to the hold swung open, and Red Chills loomed in the doorway, a lantern held high over his head. "You, lawman!"

"What's your problem, Red?"

"That money you been handing around. It's counterfeit."

"That's right."

"It ain't even *good* counterfeit."

"It was good enough to fool you stupid bastards."

With an oath, Red stormed into the hold and aimed a kick at Longarm. Longarm ducked, grabbed the man's big right foot, and twisted. Red went down hard on his back, the lantern crashing to the hold's floor. Its flame winked out. In the sudden darkness, Longarm gained a slight advantage and began to pound the wildly thrashing mountain man.

Reaching back for the lantern, Longarm brought its base down on the side of Red's face. Red flopped convulsively. Longarm lifted his crude weapon a second time and brought it down with even greater force on the man's skull. This time the big man lay perfectly still.

Longarm was searching the unconscious man's pockets for a weapon when two others stormed into the hold. One of them kicked Longarm in the gut while his companion dragged Red's body out of the hold. Before Longarm could recover, the door was slammed shut on them, and once again the three of them were alone in the smothering darkness.

●　　●　　●

How long it was before Longarm heard the side of the schooner groaning against the dock, he couldn't be sure—but it was surely more than a few hours. Frida and Jed had managed to drop off into an exhausted sleep, but they both came awake when the thud of running feet over their heads grew suddenly louder.

A moment later the door was flung open and the three of them were led out. When they reached the main deck, they found it was early morning. But there was no sunlight—only a steady, drenching rain. Looking beyond the dock, all Longarm could make out through the drifting curtains of rain were a tumble of ramshackle buildings and, hovering just beyond them, a dim pile of mountains shrouded in mist and rain.

Longarm and his companions were poked roughly into a line along the deck. As they stood there, their hands were tucked brutally behind them and then shackled. Then came a large contingent of men, already shackled, trooping up out of the schooner's bowels, their faces as grim and as dour as Longarm imagined his own to be. To his surprise, he recognized two of them. They were the same men who had been Red Chills' poker partners on that train, the ones who had joined the conductor and the engineer in chasing after him.

They were too unhappy to look about them, so neither caught sight of Longarm.

The wooden gangway was dropped onto the dock, and they were marched off the ship, through the driving rain, toward a couple of high-backed ore wagons. The two teams of draft horses stood patiently in their traces with hardly a quiver, their long, sodden tails hanging straight down. As Longarm clambered up into one of the wagons after Jed and Frida, he looked once again at the heavily timbered mountains and wondered where in blazes he was.

"That's easy enough to answer," one grizzled old-timer said. "This here is Vancouver Island. Ain't you never heard of this place before?"

Longarm shook his head.

The old man chuckled. It was really a series of hissing

sounds he made, since he had no teeth. "Neither did I, till a few hours ago," he said.

The rain did not let up as the horses pulled them deeper into the forested foothills. Everyone in the wagon with them was too miserable to speak or even notice Frida's presence; but she was the only girl, and Longarm and Jed positioned themselves on each side of her throughout the interminable ride.

They came at last to a small settlement of shacks and mine buildings, huddled in under the brow of a mountain. Glancing up at the mountain, Longarm could not see much of its flank, since most of it was lost in the heavy, moisture-laden clouds. He was so wet by this time that he felt as slick as a seal. His shirt and pants were plastered to him like a second skin, and his feet inside his boots were cold and clammy.

They left the ore wagons and were once again lined up, then forced to march up a rain-slick incline toward a large compound made up almost entirely of bunkhouses constructed of unpeeled logs and raw, unpainted pine boards. Woodsmoke hung heavily in the damp air. Beyond the buildings, in the rain-shrouded distance, Longarm could barely make out the raw slash in the side of a mountain— a mine's diggings—flanked by spidery catwalks and flumes. Everywhere Longarm looked, he saw men with sawed-off shotguns watching them carefully, the rain pouring off their hatbrims in constant, gleaming rivulets.

Frida shivered. Longarm could hear her teeth chattering. "We'll be inside soon," he told her.

The bunkhouse, when they reached it finally, had a dirt floor and a roof that leaked just about everywhere. Six men were already in there, huddled on what appeared to be the choicest bunks, with blankets wrapped about them to keep out the cold dampness. Longarm and Jed spotted an empty bunk in a far corner and secured it for Frida, after which they found bunks for themselves close by.

Every surface in the bunkhouse was sopping wet, and the interior of the place seemed even colder than the outside. There were no sheets on the straw-filled mattresses, only mildewed army blankets of a quality known to have done its share in bringing on the Indian Wars. Frida's blanket had at least three large rents in it.

They knew Frida would be better off if she could remove her wet clothes and dry herself off, then wrap the blanket around her. Frida knew this as well, but there was no question of her daring to do such a thing, as it now became fully apparent that every eye in the place was resting boldly and speculatively on the girl. Frida's presence had electrified what had been dull, cheerless men.

"Try to get some sleep, Frida," Longarm told her. "Jed and I will keep an eye out."

"I'll try," she said, her voice hoarse. She had begun to cough during the long, cold ride to this camp.

As Frida huddled into a ball and did her best to sleep, Longarm and Jed took stock of their situation.

"It's a mine," Longarm told Jed. "Looks like we're going to do some mining."

"What kind of a mine?" Jed asked.

"Gold. The same gold you watched them load onto those river steamers at Albert."

Jed considered that for a moment, then shook his head unhappily. "That's one thing I never wanted to be—a miner."

"Looks like you are one now—or will be pretty damn soon."

"I'm worried. About Frida, I mean."

"We'll just have to keep an eye out."

Jed nodded, none too confidently. "I know that."

Longarm understood the uncertainty he detected in Jed's voice. They would have to keep watch on Frida night and day if they were to be successful in keeping her out of the cruel embrace of these haggard, miserable men.

The afternoon passed slowly. Outside the dripping bunkhouse, the rain slacked off for short periods, only to commence once again, seemingly with redoubled fury. By nightfall, the rain was pounding down on the roof with such force that they did not hear the approach of the day's miners until the men quartered in their bunkhouse began pouring into it. Peering out through a grimy window, Longarm saw the bulk of the miners filing past into the other bunkhouses. He estimated that there were more than forty men in all.

This was no small-time operation, and Longarm was anxious to meet the man behind it—if he lived long enough.

A Chinese gong woke them for breakfast. Longarm sat up and looked out. The rain had stopped, but a thick, luminous fog hung over the meadows and trees that crowded hard upon the compound. He heard the men around him cursing and pulling on their britches, as they left their bunks and stumbled out into the fog-shrouded morning.

Longarm and Jed waited until Frida was ready, then left the bunkhouse with her. It was meant to save her from the ribald comments and stares of the other men, but it did not achieve the desired effect. The whistles and catcalls—not to mention the cruel comments concerning her evident ability to satisfy both of her escorts—enraged Longarm and Jed, but both saw at once the futility of trying to take on the entire work force and managed to maintain expressionless faces.

The mine's guards marched them off toward a long cookshack that had been built on the margin of the camp under a stand of very tall pines. In single file, they picked up their trays and passed the Chinese cooks who ladled out their steaming oatmeal, salt pork, and molten coffee.

They had to eat standing, huddled under the pines for protection. The guards were positioned close by, their shotguns cradled in their arms. Beside Longarm, Frida began coughing. He took the tin plate from her.

"I can't eat it," she said. "It's terrible."

"How do you feel?"

"Miserable."

Longarm was about to throw the contents of Frida's breakfast onto the ground when that same old man who had spoken to him on the trip to the mine grabbed his arm.

"If'n that girl don't want hers, I'll take it," he said eagerly.

Longarm shrugged and handed the plate to him. But as

the man started to devour the salt pork and porridge, another man came up suddenly from behind and spun him around.

"You don't have no right to hers!" he screamed, outraged. "She has to take that back if she don't want it, so's the rest of us can have seconds!"

Another irate miner joined this one, and together they wrested the plate from the old man. Longarm had seen enough. He spun the first man around, caught him on the jaw with a sledging blow, then waded into the second one. With a roar, the rest of the miners joined in the battle, while Jed hastily backed Frida away from the roiling mass of bodies.

The guards broke it up finally by wading into the melee and clubbing every head in reach. The sound of cracking skulls brought most of the men back to order, and a few shots into the air completed their lesson. The battered miners parted sullenly. Longarm, still on the ground under two burly men, was let up.

As he got to his feet and looked around him, he saw the old man lying on the ground a few feet from him. Someone had trampled on his head, crushing it. His skull looked like an enormous eggshell that had been cracked for breakfast. Longarm looked away.

The biggest of the guards approached Longarm.

"You the one started this?"

"No," Longarm said, pointing to the old man with the broken skull. "He was."

"I'm lookin' for the lawman. You be him?"

Longarm nodded. "That's me."

The man smiled lazily. He had a long nose and not much of a chin. His eyes were red-rimmed and eager. He brought the butt of his shotgun around suddenly and caught Longarm on the side of his face. Longarm went down on one knee, blinked away the pain, and considered coolly whether or not he wanted to kill the bastard. He decided he didn't—not right then.

"You through with me, you son of a bitch?"

"Sure. I'm through with you. But the boss ain't. He wants to see you."

"Where is he?"

"Start moving. I'll take you to him. But you keep your distance, lawman."

With Longarm in the lead, and the gunman keeping close behind him with his shotgun trained on Longarm's back, they left the compound and climbed a hill, passed through a small patch of timber, and came out onto a meadow. A path led through the meadow to a large white mansion on a small rise. The mansion looked to be at least a half-mile distant, and Longarm could see the evergreen shrubbery that fronted the spacious building, and the well-kept grounds leading up to it.

Before they reached the mansion itself, however, Longarm was led into a gardener's cottage on the estate's grounds. Waiting inside for Longarm was a man standing in front of a couple of wooden cartons that served as his desk. The stock of his shotgun was resting on the floor, its barrel propped back against the side of one of the cartons. A well-oiled sixgun was riding on his right hip. Leaning back against one of the cartons, he crossed his arms and regarded Longarm with a mixture of curiosity and contempt.

He was a tall man with a black patch over his right eye, a crooked tilt to his broad shoulders, and a livid scar that ran back from his right eye socket all the way to his ear. Longarm's first thought was that this must be the ugliest son of a bitch he had ever seen.

His second thought was that he knew indisputably who this man was. From the description he had read of him—a description he himself had followed earlier when he and Vail had decided Longarm should impersonate him—Longarm realized he was standing at last in front of the *real* Wolf Caulder.

And it was the man's *right* eye, not his left, that had the patch over it.

"So you're Wolf Caulder," Longarm said needlessly.

"That's right. And you'd be that deputy U.S. marshal —the one they call Longarm."

Longarm nodded.

"Heard you was on my tail," Caulder said, his broken face lit suddenly with a sardonic smile. "You sure as hell are a hard man to lose." He shook his head admiringly. "Well, you found me—only it ain't goin' to do you much good."

Longarm did not see what response he could make to that, so he said nothing. Caulder grabbed his shotgun by its barrel and stepped away from the crates.

"I'm supposed to take you up to the big house. This jasper you're goin' to meet, Longarm, is a queer duck— but I don't want you takin' any shots at him, if you know what I mean. He's a foreigner with strange ways, but he knows how to treat them as works for him."

"I noticed that this morning, during breakfast—and last night in that fine bunkhouse where your boss put us up."

"Them are workers. We can't put them up in hotels, now, can we? We do the best we can, what with squint cooks and all."

"That's a lot of horseshit, Caulder," Longarm said harshly, remembering the conditions Frida and the rest had had to sleep through the night before. "And you and this boss of yours know it. These men aren't working here because they want to. It's slavery, and you're a part of it."

Caulder's face hardened and he leaned close. "Go ahead, lawman. Go ahead. Just keep talking like that, and you'll have me stuffing the muzzle of this Greener down your throat."

"Shove it up your ass, Caulder. And take me to this maniac in charge. I'd like to meet the son of a bitch. Does he have a name?"

"Sir Allen Pembroke, he is—and you'll learn soon enough. He's a strange one, like I said, but he ain't no son of a bitch and he ain't no maniac, less'n you rile him."

Longarm recognized the name at once; it was the name Jed had seen on the export-import office door, back in Squamish. "I'll try to remember that," Longarm drawled.

They left the cottage and walked across a well-tended lawn, up the broad steps to the porch, and then followed the veranda around to the side of the house until they came to a door. Caulder knocked on it once, shortly, then stepped back and told Longarm to open it and go inside.

Longarm did as he was instructed and found himself in a spacious, elegantly furnished room, with imposing portraits of landed gentry staring imperiously down from the walls. A huge fireplace took up one wall, with a crackling fire glowing in its belly—a welcome warmth after the clammy dampness outside. Trophies of bear, elk, and mountain goat crowded the wall over the fireplace's mantle and, below them, superb rifles were hung in a display almost as brilliant.

Standing before the fireplace was the Englishman, Sir Allen Pembroke—a queer duck, indeed, just as Caulder had warned. He was wearing slippers, skintight dark trousers, a red velvet dinner jacket, and a high, stiff collar that would have choked the life out of Longarm. A wine-colored cravat was tied neatly at his throat. His gray hair was thinning, and he wore it slicked straight back over his freckled skull. Tucked into one eye socket was a gleaming, silver-framed monocle. His nose was long and slender, his chin slightly receding. In build, the man was exceedingly thin and drawn. He looked as if all that would be needed to sweep him away would be a strong breeze—until one caught the iron gleam in his small, dark eyes.

Behind him, Caulder closed the door, then nudged Longarm closer to Pembroke.

"This is that lawman you wanted," Caulder drawled. "You want me to stay?"

"Is he armed?"

"No, sir, he ain't."

"Then wait outside on the porch, Caulder."

Longarm heard the man close the door behind him.

Sir Allen Pembroke came toward Longarm, his right hand outstretched. He seemed almost overjoyed to see the lawman.

Astonished, Longarm shook Sir Allen's hand. The fellow's grip, he found, was surprisingly robust, if not downright friendly.

"Sit down, Deputy," the man said eagerly. "Sit down,

by all means. This is quite a pleasure for me."

The chair Pembroke indicated was a wing-backed Morris chair. Longarm settled gingerly into it. He was not quite sure how to take all this, but he was grateful for the consideration.

"This sure as hell ain't been a pleasure for *me*, Pembroke."

"Of course, of course. I fully understand your feeling on this matter. All I can do is apologize and say how much I regret the inconvenience all this has cost you and your friends. My agents are tenacious on my behalf, but at times show lamentable judgment. You have, however, been rather harsh on my agents, as I now understand it. And paying us off in counterfeit money. That really was most unfair."

"Was it? What are you paying those poor devils out there working your mine?"

"Excellent wages, Deputy. Excellent. I am keeping it in trust for them, though—and once this mine has played out, they will be handsomely rewarded. A bank in Vancouver is holding each man's wages in trust for him. They will be rich men, all—when that time comes."

"If it ever does. You sure you can trust that bank?"

"Of course. I own it." The man leaned solicitously over Longarm. "Now tell me. Is there anything I can get for you, Deputy?"

Longarm took a deep breath. What he wanted now—but knew he could not possibly get—was a cheroot from his private stock. "You wouldn't happen to have any Maryland rye around this place, would you?"

The man seemed delighted at Longarm's request. He fairly bounded over to a tassled cord hanging in a corner by the fireplace, and yanked on it. Almost immediately, it seemed, a liveried manservant appeared in the doorway. The only things that ruined the impression the fellow should have made were the two missing buttons on his braided jacket and the bulge of chewing tobacco in his cheek.

"Claude," Pembroke instructed. "A tall glass of Maryland rye. And bring the bottle."

As Claude vanished back out the door, Pembroke glanced

unhappily at Longarm. "You must forgive him, Deputy. I find I have no alternative but to make do with the raw, unlettered creatures of this miserable frontier."

"That's a rotten shame."

"It does make things difficult."

Longarm's drink arrived on a silver tray. The bottle and glass were set down without much ceremony on a highly polished table alongside Longarm's chair. Longarm poured his drink, then looked with a cocked eyebrow at his host. "Care to join me?"

"I would rather not. It is too early in the day for me. But I understand you frontiersmen have no such qualms."

"That's right," Longarm said, sipping his drink and slipping back into the chair. "Especially after the morning I've just had."

"As I said, sir, I regret that most sincerely. But now to the reason I had you brought here."

"I'm listening," Longarm said.

"I need you to help me. I do not think I can trust my guards. Indeed, I have reason to believe they are robbing me—not tallying the gold I am mining here accurately. Some of them, I am sure, are spiriting the richest gold ore away and hiding it somewhere on the island."

"You mean they are crooks," Longarm said, smiling.

"Precisely."

"What the hell did you expect? That's what you've recruited, ain't it?"

The man sighed, pulled a chair closer to Longarm, and sat down. "You must believe me when I say I had no choice. I could not get workers to stay here on this island, even after I discovered how rich the vein was. A night would come, rumors would fly, and the next thing I knew, they would be gone."

"Rumors? Rumors of what?"

"Nonsensical rumors—the hobgoblins of untutored minds, of no substance. I believe there is a tribe of aborigines, deeper in the island's interior, that raids the coastal areas occasionally. I have tried to interest my men in raising a war party of our own and flushing the red devils out, but they will have none of it. They insist that these aborigines are some kind of monstrous tribe that cannot be stopped by a white man's bullets. Sheer poppycock, but there was nothing I could do to persuade them differently."

"So you began recruiting criminals."

"Tell me, Deputy, is it such a disservice to your country if I lure your worst outlaws and killers to this island and set them to work? You are rid of them, and I am able to continue my mining operation."

Longarm sipped his drink and shrugged. "I reckon that depends. The thing is, my government wants these outlaws, these murderers, to go on trial."

"You saw them last night and this morning. Do you not think their punishment is as just—perhaps even more just— than yours?"

"I reckon you got a point, Sir Allen. But my government had no idea what was happening to them. The Justice Department thought they were escaping scot-free to South America."

"Now that you know differently, perhaps you will help me."

"Just what do you have in mind?"

"As I said, I can't trust my guards. As you remind me, they are blackguards, sir. Outlaws, outcasts, the detritus of a society run amuck."

"A society run where?"

"Your country, sir. The United States of America—a ceaseless battleground that attracts the castoffs, the riffraff of the entire world."

"I see."

"However, you are a lawman, sir—capable of dealing with these specimens of human depravity. You have come here to put a stop to my operation, no doubt. But I have a proposition, and I trust you will give it a fair hearing."

"I'm listening."

"I want you to take charge, to oversee these men for me."

"What makes you think you can trust me?"

"You are a man of the law."

"What's to prevent me from rounding these specimens

up and taking them back to the States, to jail, where they belong?"

Pembroke smiled. "I doubt they would go, Deputy. Willingly, that is. Have you considered what a merry time you would have, taking them all back in chains—or however you propose to do it."

"I admit that would be well nigh impossible, without help, that is."

"You would get none from me, Deputy—and I doubt that Wolf Caulder and any of his ilk would help, either."

"I see your point."

Pembroke leaned suddenly closer. "And have you considered what would happen to you if I were to send you back now to those miners?"

Longarm frowned. "No," he replied. "I haven't."

"Already a few of those men know who you are. Soon every man in the camp will know that you are a lawman— a deputy U.S. marshal. Can you imagine the enthusiasm with which they will approach the task of disposing of a man with your credentials—even those blackguards who are *not* on your government's list of wanted men?"

Longarm nodded. It did not take much imagination.

"Will you do it, sir? Will you take charge?"

"On one condition."

"And what's that?"

"There's a girl came with me—she's looking for her brother. I want her out of the mines and out of those damp bunkhouses. Take her in here and look after her, and I'll do what I can to help you control your workers."

"Done!" the man said, jumping to his feet and rubbing his hands together in excitement. "By George, you'll be just the one to stop this thievery! This girl—how old is she?"

"Around twenty or so. I'm not sure."

"If she can do housework and cook, she'll be most welcome in this household. My wife disappeared—ran away, I suppose—ten months ago. I have been unable to leave the island during that time to procure myself another wife. This girl will do nicely."

"Not if you're aiming to make her your wife, she won't."

"I didn't mean that, Deputy. As I said, someone to do housework and cook. That would be sufficient for now, I am sure."

Longarm was in no mood to argue with the man. He got to his feet. "I'll need weapons, and one other thing. I'll want someone I can trust to back me."

"Do you have anyone in particular in mind?"

"Yes. His name is Jed. He was taken with me."

"Done. And of course you won't mind if I have a man to back me, as well."

"That sounds reasonable enough."

"Good. I think Wolf Caulder will do nicely."

"I suggest you call in Wolf Caulder now to give him the good news. I suspicion it'd be worth something to see his reaction."

"It will at that," Pembroke said with a chuckle, as he went to the door leading out onto the veranda and opened it to call Caulder back into the room.

Chapter 9

When Longarm returned to the compound, armed—like Caulder—he found the work crews strangely buoyant; some men were even smiling as they worked. Longarm found out soon enough what had happened.

Frida had found her brother Tim.

The brawl had left the men disorganized, and when they marched off to the digs, they did not keep to their proper bunkhouse crews. The result was that Tim found himself slogging along a few yards in front of his sister. Too depressed, too weary the night before and that morning, he had paid little heed to the talk that had raced through the bunkhouses about the presence of a girl.

Frida's cry brought Tim around in his tracks, and when the news of this miracle circulated throughout the camp, the spirits of even the most hard-bitten outlaws lifted. It did not mean that they would no longer look with hungry eyes on the girl; but from now on, that hunger would be mixed with grudging admiration.

There weren't too many men there who were blessed with sisters willing to make such a journey to join their brother.

In the days that followed, Longarm learned much about Sir Allen Pembroke's situation and his phony escape route, a brilliantly successful plan he had devised for importing labor and swelling his coffers, all at the same time.

Once the Englishman had found himself unable to keep workers on the island at even the most inflated wages, he simply decided to import labor from the States on his Devil's Railroad. It had been his intent, the man told Longarm rather smugly, to "siphon off" the bad blood accumulating in the Western states.

But when Longarm inquired why Sir Allen could not keep his workers in the first place, Sir Allen told Longarm little more than he had earlier—aborigines, Indians inhabiting the thickly forested mountain slopes farther inland, were raiding the workers' living quarters and in some cases carrying off captives. But what gave these stories an air of unreality—at least as far as Longarm was concerned—was the insistence by some of the workers that this was not a tribe of Indians at all, but a tribe of giant, fur-clad mountain men instead, mountain men who gave off a stench so horrific it caused grown men to pass out.

There had been raids by these "aborigines" on the miners' compounds one moonless night less than two months before, as Longarm learned from Frida's brother. As a result, Tim insisted, the men had become even more restless than usual, especially when they realized that Sir Allen thought their fears were totally groundless. His answer to their demand that he do something had been to go off with a few of his guards, tramping through the almost impenetrable forests of the region in search of the aborigines, as he insisted on calling them.

But though Sir Allen, equipped with the latest in long-range firepower, including a newly imported telescopic sight, scoured the forests for close to a week, he returned with no scalps to add to his display over the fireplace—and a renewed contempt for the groundless fears of his men.

And there the matter remained as Longarm began to do what he could to relieve somewhat the conditions of the miners. Not that this in any way decreased his desire to turn the tables on this improbable Englishman.

Two weeks later, Longarm was ready to make his move.

"The plan is quite simple," said Longarm, leaning close to Tim and Jed. "I'll promise Wolf Caulder that he won't be prosecuted. I will allow him and all those who want to go with him to take over the schooner that brought us here and sail for parts unknown—in return for his cooperation in putting an end to Sir Allen's operation here."

"I don't reckon Wolf will go along," said Tim.

Longarm looked over at Frida's brother. Only a few years older than his sister, he was almost a duplicate of her—though perhaps a trifle leaner in the face, and with a nose just a mite larger and somewhat more crooked. Unwilling from the beginning to look upon himself as a criminal, he had fought to establish this fact with almost every fellow worker, until the men at last decided he was just too much trouble to tangle with. From that time on, they left him alone. But the scars of Tim's numerous battles—on his forehead, around his chin, not to mention the crooked pull to his nose—remained as vivid reminders of his independence of mind—and his stubborn courage.

"Why do you say that, Tim?"

"Wolf's got other ideas of his own about Sir Allen."

"You know that for a fact, do you?"

"Only what I've been hearing. But it's been going around for a spell."

"He's in a good position to do whatever he wants with that crazy son of a bitch," said Jed.

It was a Sunday afternoon. It hadn't rained for two days, and on Longarm's insistence the men had all been given the day off to complete the construction of a mess hall under the pines, large enough to shelter all of them during meals.

With commendable diligence, the men were working on it at that moment. They were eager to complete it before the interminable rain began once more.

Meanwhile, Longarm, Jed, and Tim were gathered in the gardner's cottage, around the same crates Caulder used as a makeshift desk. They were waiting for Frida. In response to Longarm's request earlier, she had been given permission by Sir Allen to visit with Tim—and to bring Longarm a bottle of Maryland rye.

As was his custom before each working day, that morning Longarm had received his instructions from Sir Allen on his front porch—with Wolf Caulder standing close beside the Englishman. Longarm, no doubt on Caulder's suggestion, had not been allowed inside Sir Allen's mansion since the day he had accepted the man's offer to oversee his workers. But Wolf Caulder—and lately, Red Chills—had recently moved into one of the rooms in back of the kitchen.

It was this fact that had prompted Jed's remark. And Jed was correct. Caulder was in the catbird seat where the Englishman was concerned.

"What we will have to do," said Tim, "is offer Caulder more than he can get by taking over this operation from Sir Allen—if that's what he's planning."

"What *they're* planning—Caulder *and* Red Chills," Jed said, glancing nervously at Longarm.

"That's some pair," admitted Longarm. He knew why Jed had glanced at him in that fashion. After Red had recovered from the beating Longarm had given him on the schooner, Chills had vowed he would kill Longarm the first chance he got.

It was undoubtedly Red's ill feeling toward Longarm that had prompted Sir Allen to make him Caulder's lieutenant.

Longarm had understood immediately Sir Allen's motive in using Caulder and Red Chills in this fashion. The Englishman was sitting on a powder keg and was trying to defuse it by pitting one cadre of guards against the other. As a result, Longarm was willing to bet that since Longarm's arrival and appointment to his present post, the filching of gold ore by Caulder or any of the other guards had fallen off considerably.

Like Longarm, they were too busy looking over their shoulders at each other.

"So what do we do?" asked Jed. "We can't stay in this place, digging gold for that madman."

"Sure we can," said Tim ironically. "That's what we've been doing for close to a year."

Jed looked at Longarm. "When are you going to approach Caulder?"

"As soon as I can. Frida will act as our go-between."

"I don't want her put in any danger, Longarm," said Tim.

Longarm looked at Frida's brother. "Tim, she hasn't been in anything *else* since she started out to find you."

There was a soft rap on the door and Frida entered. After she put down the tray containing the rye and the glasses, she hugged her brother, then looked over to flash weary but pleased smiles at Longarm and Jed.

"What's going on up there in the big house?" Jed asked her.

"Let me get my breath," said Frida, slumping down onto a wooden box and brushing an errant lock of hair off her forehead.

Longarm poured drinks all around.

"Something's up," said Frida. "I don't know what for sure—but something. And I don't trust Caulder or Red. If it wasn't for Sir Allen, I think Red would have—" She glanced nervously at her brother and shuddered slightly, and every man there knew what she meant.

"If he touches you," Tim said, his voice hushed, "I'll—"

"I know. I know," she said hastily. "But that won't make things any different—and so far, he's kept his hands to himself. I'm just saying that it's been Sir Allen that's kept him—and Wolf Caulder—in line. But I think they're planning something."

"We've been thinking the same thing," Longarm said. "Do you have any idea what it is—or when they mean to do it?"

"No I don't. I think it's just a lot of talk now. The two argue somethin' fierce, and do a lot of drinking. Sir Allen don't seem to mind, though."

Longarm smiled, nodding. "Of course he doesn't mind. With those two at each other's throats, he don't have a thing to fear from either of them. Frida, I want you to give Caulder a message for me. Can you do that?"

"Yes. I think so."

"Tell him I want to meet him later today. This afternoon, if he can get away."

"Where?"

"In here. He can bring Chills, if he wants. Tell him it's about his record in the States, and what I can do to help him."

"Help him?"

"Yes."

"Suppose he tells Sir Allen what you're planning?" asked Jed.

Longarm shrugged. "What difference does it make? I'm sure Sir Allen knows that everyone on this godforsaken island is scheming to get off. He'd be a fool to think I wouldn't try something. I'm sure he *ain't* a fool and that he expects it. If Caulder tells him, we'll just have to think of something else. The only other choice is to wait for a miracle—and I don't really expect one."

"When do you want me to tell him, Longarm?" Frida asked.

"As soon as possible."

She nodded.

"You all right up there, waiting on that crazy man, Frida?" Tim inquired.

"Yes. So far. Sir Allen has kept me pretty busy, but that's not so bad. At least it keeps me from thinking too much about this horrible place. And the rain."

"Yes," said Jed with a sigh. "The rain."

There was no comment anyone needed to add to that. The weather was the single most depressing fact about this island.

Wolf Caulder was waiting for Longarm alone. He had lit a lantern and set it down on one of the crates. Longarm pulled the door shut behind him, transferring his loaded

120

shotgun to his left hand as he did so.

Wolf was armed also. He had lain his shotgun across the top of one of the crates, its twin bores peering into Longarm's soul.

"Hold it right there, Longarm," said Wolf. "You don't need to come any closer to tell me what you got to say."

"You like it here, Caulder?"

"Not especially."

"How much is Pembroke paying you?"

"I get a dry bed and decent meals. He says something about a trust account in one of his banks, but I don't pay no attention to that."

"You've already spent a winter here. You want to do it again?"

"Get to the point, Longarm."

"Then listen, and listen good. I am offering you—and all those who want to join you—a chance to get out of this place. You can take that schooner to wherever you want to go—South America, Mexico, wherever. And you have my word that the United States Government won't come after you."

"No deal, Longarm."

Longarm shrugged wearily. He could not deny he was disappointed at this response.

"I'll tell you what I want instead."

"Name it."

"A full pardon."

"Is that all?"

"That's all. You promise me that, and I'll throw in with you."

"Suppose I can't deliver on it."

"Then I want your word that you'll help me get out of the country—that I won't have to serve time in any federal lockup."

"You mean break the law—spring you?"

"Call it whatever you want, but them's my terms."

"All right. It's a deal."

"I want your hand on it."

Longarm stepped closer to the crates. Wolf reached over

the top, and the two men shook hands.

"What the hell's in these crates, anyway?" Longarm asked.

"Furniture, paintings, all sorts of fancy stuff, for the new wing Sir Allen is planning."

Longarm shook his head. "The man is crazy."

"Maybe. Now just what have you got in mind?"

"First off, disarm Sir Allen. Go easy on him, but I want him kept under lock and key, however you do it. Then we'll give it to the workers straight. They help us take over that schooner, they can have it, as long as they transport us back across the strait. We'll need all the guards to cooperate, of course."

"And you're going to let all them outlaws escape, Longarm—sail away to South America? That don't sound like you."

"In a way, Sir Allen has a point. As long as these men stay out of the United States, what do we care what happens to them? The important thing is that we won't have to contend with this Devil's Railroad anymore—and a man running what amounts to a slave colony for his own private profit will have been stopped for good."

"What do you plan on doing to him?"

"I ain't figured that out yet. But let's eat the apple one bite at a time."

"When do you want me to move?"

"Tonight's as good a time as any. As soon as Sir Allen's in our hands, I'll parlay with the workers."

"Have you said anything to the guards?"

"I'll take care of that when I leave here."

"Then let's do it," Caulder said, with a heartiness that indicated he had just made his decision and was willing to live with it. "I don't mind telling you, this has been one crazy year for me—not at all what I had in mind when I set out for South America."

"There's just one thing more," Longarm said.

"I'm listening."

"Red Chills. Are you sure he'll go along?"

"He'll go along."

"What did you and him have in mind, Caulder—before I spoke to you just now, I mean."

Caulder frowned. "I don't know what you mean."

"Cut the horseshit. The whole camp knows you and Chills had something planned."

Caulder shrugged. "It ain't nothin' we settled on for sure, Longarm. Just something we been thinking on."

"If Red decides to cause trouble, he could do it. I figure he don't exactly think of me as his favorite lawman."

Caulder allowed himself a slight smile. "And I guess he's got his reasons, sure enough."

"All right, Caulder. I'll let you handle Red. But make sure you do, or all bets are off."

Longarm turned and walked to the door. His hand on the doorknob, he looked back at Caulder. "Go easy on this crazy Englishman, Caulder, but get a handle on him. He's wily, so don't let him talk you out of anything. When you've made your move, send Frida down to the camp with the news."

Caulder nodded.

Longarm left.

The mess hall was almost completed. The roof was up, and the back and one side were finished. The men were using unpeeled pine logs, but the work was neat; the walls appeared solid.

As Longarm noted how well the men had worked this Sunday, he wondered for a crazy moment if he was doing the right thing in breaking up Sir Allen's operation. This motley crew of outlaws, murderers, and highwaymen had shown a grudging ability to work together for a common goal. Longarm could not help but notice the camaraderie that seemed to have developed even between the most bloodthirsty of antagonists. It was almost too bad he had to bring this rare conviviality to an end.

There was still enough light left to get a good deal more work done. Longarm told Jed to call together the guards. When they were all gathered, Longarm drew them off some distance from the men working on the mess hall and outlined his plan. To a man, the guards agreed to it, especially when Longarm told them what he proposed concerning the Englishman's schooner.

"How do we know we can trust you?" one of the guards asked.

"Would you rather trust to luck?"

The man nodded unhappily. "Guess that's right," he said. "We ain't been able to get anything started ourselves." He looked warily around him at his fellow guards. "Each one of us was too damn anxious not to let anyone else in on the goodies."

"You realize, with this plan of mine, you won't be able to get back here and dig up that ore you or your fellows stashed."

Another guard spoke up then. He was standing just in front of Jed. "How'd you know about that, Deputy?"

"Sir Allen," Longarm replied. "He's known all along. That's why he put me in charge of you."

The guard shook his head. "He's a real son of a bitch, that one. I'm with you, Deputy. Count me in."

That ended the discussion.

Tim was the first to see Frida approaching. She was still wearing her apron, and her face was flushed with excitement.

"Caulder told me to get you," Frida told Longarm. "He says he's got Sir Allen. He says to tell the rest of the workers. We're getting out of here!"

Frida could hardly contain herself. She hugged Tim exuberantly. Tim was just as pleased. "You want me to tell the men?" he asked Longarm.

"Yes. You tell them. I'll get the guards. The thing is, we don't want this to turn into a riot. We need these men to help us get that schooner—and we can't just let them run wild on us, once we tell them Sir Allen's in our custody."

Tim nodded soberly. "Yeah," he said. "I see what you mean. We'd be going from bad to worse, sure enough."

But there was not too much sign of that a moment later when Tim—with Longarm, Jed, and the rest of the guards looking on, their loaded shotguns resting in the crooks of their arms—made his announcement. At first there was shocked silence as each man took in the significance of Tim's words; but then a great, shuddering shout of joy rang out as men threw their hats into the air, while others began dancing and capering about like schoolboys.

But the celebration, though uninhibited, was over somewhat quickly as the men quieted, nudged each other, and looked warily back at Tim. Where a moment before Longarm had seen only unrestrained joy, now he saw some puzzlement—suspicion, even. These hard-bitten men saw the need to examine this apparent good fortune a bit more closely.

They began asking Tim questions, and that was when Longarm stepped forward to explain what he had in mind.

When he had finished, one of the men suggested they burn the bunkhouses, including the now nearly completed mess hall. Another man wanted to march immediately on the mansion and string up Sir Allen by his short hair. But both men were shouted down as Longarm insisted they were not home free, not yet.

They would have to organize themselves in preparation for the long trip back to the coast, where they would then have to take over Sir Allen's port complex, then board and capture the schooner when it returned for more ore. All this, Longarm reminded them, would take organization and leadership.

"You electin' yourself to that post, lawman?" someone shouted.

"You see anyone better qualified?"

"Just remember, you better not cross us. There's more of us than there is of you!"

"I realize that," Longarm told the man. "Do you want this job?"

"Hell, no. Lead the way, lawman. Right now you got the best hand in this here game."

"All right, then. Let's go."

With the men at his back, Longarm reached Sir Allen's mansion not long after. As the crowd surged about the veranda like an angry flood, Longarm, Frida, Jed, and Tim mounted the steps and moved around to the side door leading into the living room.

Longarm had expected Caulder to step out onto the porch to greet them. When he didn't, Longarm began to feel a trifle uneasy, though he said nothing to the others.

Longarm glanced back at the crowd of men peering up at him, then knocked and entered the room with Jed and Tim.

The room was dim and clammy. There was no fire in the fireplace. Caulder was sitting in the chair where Longarm had sat during that interview a few days before. Feeling a little better about things—his shotgun at the ready, however, just in case—Longarm stepped aside as the others filed in, then closed the door.

He turned to Caulder. "Where's Red? The men are outside, ready to get on the move to the coast. The ore wagons are being hitched up."

Caulder did not respond. Longarm hurried across the dim room to Caulder and pulled up short. Caulder's shirtfront was shiny with blood, and there appeared to be an enormous depression where the man's chest should have been—the effects, undoubtedly, of a shotgun blast—both barrels. Even as Longarm reached for the man, Caulder pitched forward lifelessly out of the chair.

Frida screamed.

Chapter 10

Longarm turned. Red Chills was standing in the doorway, a grim Sir Allen Pembroke standing beside him. The shotgun in Red's hands was pointing at Longarm, his finger tightening on the trigger.

Longarm dove behind the chair just as both barrels detonated. He felt the chair slam back against him as the buckshot hit it. Without aiming too carefully, he fired back. Both barrels went wild.

"Hold it, Longarm!" Tim cried. "Red's got Frida!"

Turning, Longarm saw Frida being dragged, struggling, through the doorway by Red Chills. As Red ducked out of sight, Sir Allen remained in the doorway.

"Give me your weapons, all of you," Pembroke said, "or I'll let Red have his way with the girl."

Jed dropped his own shotgun as Longarm got up and followed suit. Tim had not been armed.

"Now get back out there," Sir Allen said, "and tell those

127

damn fools to get that mess hall finished." He smiled. "I can smell rain coming."

Longarm led the way toward the door. Before he reached it, he looked back at Sir Allen. "You realize that if anything happens to Frida, there'll be nothing to stop us—nothing."

"You have my word, Deputy," Sir Allen said, his smile fading somewhat. "Nothing will happen to Frida as long as you keep those men working. Oh, by the way. There'll be no more Sundays off—seems it gives you too many ideas."

Longarm left the mansion to tell the men that he had been right. They were not home yet.

From that moment on, the men in the camp were united as one. Tim's sister had suddenly become the only thing outside of themselves that any of them had ever really cared about.

Longarm and the other guards were no longer allowed to carry live ammunition in their weapons. But it made no difference to the men, who worked sullenly but steadily. They dug at the hillsides and trundled the ore to the chutes in a steady stream. The rain began again, just as Sir Allen had promised, but they slogged through it without murmuring. They did all this as long as every day—on Longarm's insistence—Frida, in the company of a well-guarded Red Chills, was brought to the now completed mess hall during suppertime for a brief meeting with her brother and the rest of the men. At sight of her, the restless men would quiet, their spirits rising perceptibly; and in sheer over-abundance of good cheer, they sometimes broke out in exuberant brawls.

The two men that now served as Red Chills' bodyguard were the same two that Chills had been playing poker with on the train. Chills had plucked them from the work force, and they obviously welcomed their new employment, even though every other man in the camp regarded them—along with Red Chills—as traitors.

Frida thanked Yang Lee and leaned back in her chair while he cleared off her place. She always had to restrain herself from attempting to help him. It was something she wanted

128

to do very much. It would be such a relief if she could do something in this huge place to help out instead of sitting around all day long, a well-kept prisoner needed for daily display before the men working in the camp below.

As the Chinaman carried her dishes back to the kitchen, she pushed her chair back and got up hopefully. Surely now Red Chills would send her down to the mess hall to visit with Tim. It was later, much later than he usually sent her. And surely Red knew that he would have to send her soon, or there would be trouble.

"Sit down," said Red, his voice menacing.

Red's two bodyguards and Sir Allen both looked over at Red in some surprise. He had been as silent as a stone during the entire meal. This was the first time he had addressed anyone.

"You heard me," Red repeated to Frida. "Sit back down. You ain't going nowhere tonight."

"But...but why?" Frida asked, slumping back into her chair. "You know it will cause trouble."

He smiled, causing her to shudder involuntarily. "I'm sick of keeping you at arm's length, woman. And soon I won't have to. When that brother and his friends come storming up here to see where you're hiding, I'll be waiting for them. We'll cut them to ribbons." He glanced at his two companions. "Right?"

"I sure hope so, Red," said one of them.

"You know so. There ain't no weapon more deadly than a sawed-off at ten paces. After the first six or so go down, the rest will get the lesson in a big fat hurry. And one of those six is going to be that deputy marshal."

The man was almost licking his chops at the prospect of killing Longarm.

"You haven't bothered to consult me, I see," said Sir Allen.

"That's right."

"I do not like what you are planning. You might as well know, I will not allow it."

"Now just how in blazes are you going to stop me, you half-witted English bastard?"

At once Sir Allen was on his feet, moving quickly away

from the table. Red got up so fast that his chair went over. Sir Allen reached into his vest for something. Without waiting to find out what it was, Red stepped swiftly closer to Sir Allen and clubbed him on the head with the barrel of his sixgun.

He hit him not once, but twice. And very hard. Sir Allen crumpled to the floor.

At the same time behind her, she heard the sudden crash of dishes and the high, excited jabber of Yang Lee and his helper. A second later the kitchen door slammed open. A chill blast of air swept through the open door into the dining room.

A blast of air and a strange, unpleasant scent, worse than skunk.

"Come here, sweetheart," Red Chills said, stepping over Sir Allen's prostrate form and starting for her. "No sense in you being shy anymore. I know it's just an act. I promise you, I'll treat you just right."

Frida darted from the room, but Red was surprisingly agile for a man his size and he caught up with her in the kitchen doorway. She ducked away from him, but he crushed her to him and tried to plant a kiss on the side of her face.

"Watch it, Red!" cried one of his men.

Red turned.

To Frida's astonishment, Sir Allen was on his feet, lunging angrily toward Red. Red flung Frida from him and turned to meet the man's charge. Frida could not bear to see what Red would do to Sir Allen. She turned and raced through the kitchen. But as she started out the door, a huge form blocked her way. In the darkness she couldn't see who it was; all she could think was that it was too big to be an Indian. It was certainly not one of the men—and the stench of it smote her like a fist.

She recoiled, screaming. The huge form ducked back out of the doorway, her scream seeming to cut at it like a whip. Turning, Frida bolted through the cellar door and down the stairs.

•　　•　　•

Darkness was coming swiftly when Longarm heard Tim call to him from outside the bunkhouse. Longarm left his bunk and stepped outside. Tim was pointing at someone running toward the compound from the direction of the big house.

Looking closer, Longarm saw that it was Yang Lee, Sir Allen's Chinese cook. The sight of the running figure alerted the entire camp, since Frida had not appeared that evening at supper; and the men—not to mention Tim and Longarm—were in a nervous, surly mood. As Yang Lee entered the compound, the men closed eagerly about the Chinaman, only to find he could not speak a word of English. But after a frantic use of sign language, the men were able to get some idea of what had happened.

Red Chills had finally turned on his English lord and master.

They could not tell for sure whether Sir Allen was dead or not, but from what Longarm and the others were able to gather from the near-hysterical cook, there was little doubt that Sir Allen was under Red's control; and when Tim tried to find out about Frida, the cook simply became more hysterical.

After that, there was no need for Longarm to issue an order. As one solid mass, they left the compound and surged toward the mansion, each man carrying a weapon of some kind—an ax, a blacksmith's tongs, wrecking bars, hammers, chains, shovels. Against sawed-off shotguns, these weapons might well prove tragically inadequate, Longarm realized, but not one man seemed bothered enough by this fact to turn back.

Longarm carried an ax, Tim a claw hammer. Jed had sharpened a case knife.

It was not until they neared the mansion that the smell hit them. It struck them with the force of a physical blow.

"My God! What the hell is that?" asked Jed in amazement.

Tim shuddered. "Them damn mountain men!" he said in sudden awe. "Jesus, what a time for *them* to show up!"

The others had caught the stench as well. Almost as one man, they wavered in their tracks and looked over at Longarm—as if to catch his reaction as well, it seemed. Longarm forced himself to continue on through the oppressive, evil-smelling night, hoping that soon he would leave behind a stench that seemed to have fallen over the land like a curse.

The big house loomed out of the black night just ahead of them. Lights appeared to be blazing in all the downstairs rooms. There was just a chance, Longarm realized, that Red might not have known that the Chinese cook had alerted the men to what he had done.

But certainly he must have been aware that by not allowing Frida to see her brother that night during the supper hour, he was asking for trouble. Longarm pulled up suddenly. Of course Red knew it. And that was precisely why he had kept Frida from coming down to the mess hall.

This bold, precipitate action on the part of the men was exactly what Red wanted. It would not be long before they walked into a barrage of shotgun fire.

"Hold it!" Longarm cried. "Get down! All of you! And stay down!"

Grudgingly, muttering among themselves, the men hunkered down in the tall, already wet grass.

Longarm told Tim and Jed to circulate among the men and tell them that he was sure they were walking into a trap, and to urge them to stay put while he approached the house to check out the situation. As soon as he found out what Chills was up to, he would get back to them.

"I want to go with you," said Tim. "That's my sister in there with that son of a bitch."

"Sorry, Tim. I can't wait. Tell the men what I just said, and stay put. That means both of you, as well."

Keeping low, Longarm slipped through the grass until he reached the lawn in front of the house. Changing direction swiftly, he cut toward the gardener's house.

Just in time.

Both barrels of a shotgun opened up on him from a clump of evergreen shrubs just to the right of the porch steps. Longarm felt the buckshot whistle past him as he ducked behind the gardener's cottage. He did not pause. Running at full tilt, he circled the cottage and approached the veranda from the rear. Jumping up onto the edge of the deck, he vaulted swiftly over the railing just as Red stepped around the corner of the veranda and brought up his shotgun.

Longarm kept going, put his head and shoulders down, and flung himself through a window into the living room. In an explosion of shattered glass and broken sash, he landed on the carpeted floor only inches from the fireplace. Ashes were glowing in the fire bed—shedding just enough light to enable him to see another dark figure stepping cautiously into the room from an adjoining hallway.

Throwing himself to the floor, Longarm rolled over just as the crouching figure let loose a blast at the spot where he had been a second before. Rolling over again, Longarm jumped up and flung his ax across the room at his assailant. He heard the man's startled grunt as it struck him, then charged across the room, buried his shoulder in the man's gut, and slammed him against the wall. The fellow offered no resistance. Longarm stepped back and let him slide down the wall to the floor.

That was when he saw with some astonishment that he had buried the ax blade in the man's forehead. He pulled out the blade and leaned closer.

It was not Red Chills, but one of his two henchmen.

Dropping the bloody ax to the floor, he snatched up the shotgun and ransacked the man's pockets for ammunition. Pocketing a handful of buckshot shells, he relieved the dead man of his sixgun and stuck it in his belt.

One down, two to go.

Longarm looked out through the windows, watching for any shadows. But there was no moon, so there was little chance that if Red Chills was still out there, he would cast much of a shadow. Longarm caught no movement, heard no squeaking of boards. In fact, after those two shotgun blasts, the house and grounds were preternaturally quiet.

But there was still that clinging, fearsome stench—like a mountain man that had never changed his longjohns or taken a bath in his life—an entire herd of them!

If anything, the awesome smell had increased, causing the hair on the back of Longarm's neck to rise as he slipped silently into the hallway from which his most recent assailant had come. There was another room leading off it, from under the door of which a thin sliver of light could be seen. He moved past it and heard, coming from below his feet, muffled pounding—and the occasional cry of a girl.

Frida! She was in the cellar!

Longarm kept going and blundered into the darkened kitchen, almost fired on a crouching Chinaman, then hurried on past him to the cellar door. He had no light, but once he had descended the stairs, he let the pounding and Frida's frantic cries guide him. He came to a door that led into what appeared to be a root cellar, lifted the wooden bar, and pulled open the door.

Peering into the pitch-black interior, he said, "Frida! You all right?"

Frida exploded into his arms.

He held her tightly for a moment, then asked her, "Where's Sir Allen?"

"Upstairs," she replied, still clinging to him. "Holed up in his bedroom. He's armed, Longarm. He's got one of his high-powered rifles with him."

"What happened?"

"Red struck Sir Allen on the head with his sixgun. I thought he had killed him, so I ran into the kitchen, but as Red came after me, Sir Allen got up from the floor and pulled Red down from behind. Then...." She shuddered. "Then I ran down here."

"But who locked you in?"

"Red Chills. He came after me and found me. He said he had Sir Allen locked in his room and he didn't care how many high-powered rifles he had, it wouldn't stop Red from wringing his neck when the time came. And then he locked me in here. He said I'd keep nicely until he was ready for me."

"Maybe you'd better stay down here until the men and me can take care of Red and his crony. The whole camp's outside now, waiting to charge this place."

"Oh, Longarm! Please! Don't leave me down here alone in this place! Please! take me with you."

Longarm caught the abject terror in her voice and relented at once. "All right. Here. Take this pistol."

She took it from him gratefully. Then, with Longarm in the lead, the two of them moved back up the stairs to the kitchen. The Chinaman that Longarm had almost killed a moment before was gone, out the still-open kitchen door, Longarm had no doubt.

"That smell, Longarm! What is it?"

"Mountain men—and not very clean ones, at that. Those aborigines Sir Allen couldn't find are somewhere nearby, it looks like."

"I *saw* one, Longarm! In that doorway! Only it wasn't any mountain man. It couldn't have been. He was so big!"

"Red's a big man, Frida. He's a mountain man and he's still loose. Come on."

They slipped cautiously into the next room, paused, then darted through it.

"Where's the stairs to the second floor?" Longarm asked.

"This way," Frida said.

She led him down a dark hallway, then up a broad spiral staircase. They were almost at the second-floor landing when, glancing down, Longarm saw someone move out of the shadows at the foot of the stairs.

"Down!" he shouted to Frida as he flung himself around and emptied both barrels at the shadowy figure below. Longarm heard a horrific bellow as the man he hit flung his arms up, spun about, and charged back through the dark hallway.

"One more to go," Longarm said, as he turned and continued on up the stairs, dropping shells into his open shotgun.

"Sir Allen!" Longarm cried. "It's the deputy! I've got Frida! You'd better get out of here and come with me."

At once, a door at the end of the hallway was flung open. Longarm saw the Englishman's frail figure outlined in the doorway, a gleaming rifle in his hand.

"Drop it!" Longarm said.

"No. You drop yours. You just shot off both barrels, and I didn't hear you reload."

135

Longarm snapped shut his shotgun. "Hell, man," he said to the Englishman, "this is no time to dicker. Get out of here with me while you've still got the chance. Red Chills will kill you the first opportunity he gets."

"And the workers outside—those uncivilized wretches I shanghaied onto this island—what of them? How do you think they would welcome me?"

"I'll take care of you."

"I don't believe you. And if I did, I would be a fool. There's no way now that any man can keep that pack from my throat."

"Put down that rifle, Sir Allen," Longarm persisted. "And come with me!"

"No!"

"All right. Let that be your decision."

He turned and led Frida down the stairs. Before they reached the first floor, they heard the sound of a window shattering as a stone crashed through it. Then came the crash of another window breaking, and yet another. From outside came the dim roar of angry men, no longer willing to wait for Longarm.

Longarm caught a strong whiff of kerosene and realized that at least one of the missiles had probably broken an oil lamp. A second later there was a loud *whomp* from the room adjoining the hall, and great orange tongues of flame suddenly erupted in the doorway.

Holding his arm up before his face to protect it, Longarm led Frida across the entrance hall toward the big front door. Before he could reach it, however, the door burst open and in charged Tim and Jed, the rest of the men on their heels.

At sight of Longarm with Frida, the men pulled up in confusion. In a moment the hallway was a confusion of milling bodies, lit by the garish flames that were now rapidly engulfing the stairwell behind Longarm.

"Get out of here!" cried Longarm. "This house is going up!"

The men turned and tried to get back out through the narrow doorway, but some fell, and others stumbled over them. Almost at once, it seemed, a pile of bodies had trapped the rest of them in the entranceway.

"This way!" Longarm told Tim and Jed, as he dragged Frida after him through another doorway into a room that had not yet been touched by the flames. The smoke was thick, however. Longarm's eyes smarted and breathing became difficult. It felt as if there were razor blades in his chest. He plunged on blindly through the smoke-filled darkness and became aware, suddenly, of two looming forms on his right.

He glanced in that direction just as the door ahead of them burst open. Standing in the doorway was a huge figure, screaming, his entire form blazing. The man whirled in agony, striking out wildly as he flung himself into the room.

That was when Longarm saw more clearly the other two looming figures standing by the wall but he could not credit his senses, and he did not have the time to look any closer.

Meanwhile the blazing, fur-clad mountain man was not dousing the flames that enveloped him as he rolled over and over on the floor. Instead, he was spreading the fire to every corner of the room. Longarm plunged past the rolling figure and out through the door.

He found himself once again in the living room where he had flung himself through the window. He opened the door and bolted out onto the veranda. The clear air was a blessing—but not that awesome stench that still hung like a curse over the mansion.

The four of them jumped down off the veranda and headed away from the blazing mansion, a staggering, coughing stream of men following after them. They reached the gardener's cottage and pulled up.

The night was lit by the roaring inferno. As Longarm watched, he saw the figures of men on fire leaping out through windows. Sir Allen was up there somewhere on the second floor. There was a balcony, and perhaps the Englishman would be able to drop to the ground safely from it. But as the flames mounted into the sky, enveloping the mansion's roof with a sudden, crackling roar, bits of flaming debris were sent soaring into the sky until it was filled with millions of tiny red eyes.

"Where's that son of a bitch, Red Chills?" Tim asked Longarm.

"I haven't seen him since he tried to cut me down earlier on the porch."

"You think maybe he's in there with Sir Allen?"

"I don't know, Tim. But the best thing for us now is to get back to the camp, harness up those horses to the ore wagons, and get the hell out of here."

"I say we wait," said Tim. "To make sure of Red Chills and those other two with him."

Before Longarm could respond, a swarm of fur-clad giants lumbered into view from around the burning mansion. They appeared to be armed with clubs of some kind and moved with deadly effect among the crowd of dazed men who had just escaped the blazing building. Longarm heard the men's screams as these giant aborigines, or whatever the hell they were, vented their rage on the hapless men.

No more than a handful of miners had escaped the mansion with Longarm. As Frida clung to Longarm, these few men pulled back in horror at the scene they were witnessing. Not one of them—armed as poorly as they were—seemed at all anxious to come to the aid of their fellow miners.

In the garish light thrown by the now completely engulfed mansion, Longarm watched numbly as the infuriated giants lifted the men over their heads and flung them back into the blazing house. Those who were conscious screamed in sheer terror as they felt themselves being flung through the air. With shattering suddenness, their screams died the moment they disappeared into the flames. Some fell short of the blazing inferno and tried to crawl away, but they did not get far, as the mountain men pounced on them and finished them off.

Longarm was reminded of children he had seen once, trampling and beating a nest of snakes to death with sticks.

"All right," said Tim wearily. "You're right, Longarm. Let's get out of here. If Red's in that, he sure as hell won't get far."

"Look!" said Jed, pointing.

Longarm grunted as he saw what Jed was pointing at. A small band of these fearsome aborigines had spotted them and was sweeping toward them from the other side of the burning mansion.

"Get back to the compound and hitch up those ore wagons," said Longarm to Tim. "I've got something to use on these bastards. And I'm kind of looking forward to it."

Only Frida protested, but soon she and her brother were moving hurriedly off through the night with Jed and the others, while Longarm checked his shotgun load. He had taken back from Frida the sixgun he had let her have. He checked the loads in this weapon as well, and then tucked it carefully into his belt.

The blazing mansion was losing some of its fire, and the light from it was fading fast. The crackling roar of the flames had lessened considerably, and now Longarm could hear the fearsome cries and groaning of the men littering the groun about the mansion. Yet still the great, ungainly creatures moved among the fallen men and continued to assail them—as if unable to satisfy their bloodlust once it had been aroused.

As the darkness fell over this nightmarish landscape once again, Longarm moved out from the protection of the gardener's cottage to meet the great, hulking creatures trotting eagerly toward him.

Chapter 11

It was their smell that made Longarm fire—sooner than he might have otherwise. His first barrel nearly took the head off the nearest, and his second caught the overstuffed jasper beside him in the middle. But it didn't slow the rest of them down at all.

Breaking the shotgun, he slipped two more rounds in, snapped the barrels back, and fired—all in one motion— at two of the other bastards looming over him. His first barrel caught another one in the head, exploding it into a bloody shrapnel of bone, brains, and fur. Longarm ducked to one side and fired his second barrel, catching another one low. He stumbled, grabbed his crotch with both hands, then peeled forward into the grass.

The remaining mountain men pulled up, momentarily intimidated by the sight of their companions—or what was left of them—thrashing about in the grass. But they gained heart as more of their number joined them, and started once again for Longarm.

During the pause, Longarm had been able to load up again. He waited as long as he dared and fired at the nearest two, stopping only one of them. The rest—there were at least ten of them by now—spread out to encircle him, then began to close the circle.

Two rapid rifle shots rang out from Longarm's left. Two mountain men slipped to the ground. A rapid series of rifle shots followed, and the encircling band broke in confusion, as one after another of them staggered to their knees or dropped heavily to the ground.

"This way, Deputy!" shouted Sir Allen.

Longarm looked in the direction of the shout. He saw Sir Allen rise up out of the grass, a gleaming rifle in his hand.

"Hurry up! The woods are full of these damned aborigines!"

Longarm trotted toward him.

"I suppose I should say thanks," Longarm said, when he reached the Englishman.

"It would be fitting, at that. But you can thank me in a more concrete fashion, if you want."

"How?"

"You promised to protect me from the men. I think I may need that protection to get out of this alive."

"Like I said before, I'll do what I can."

"That's good enough for me. Where are the others?"

"The ones that are left, you mean?"

"Yes."

"At the compound, getting some ore wagons ready to move out."

"I suggest we join them. We'll be needed to ride shotgun, I am afraid."

As the men hurried through the night, Longarm asked the Englishman how he had managed to escape the burning mansion. As Longarm had suspected, he had tied sheets together and used them to drop from the rear balcony. The only thing that appeared to have upset him was the loss of his other big-game guns—especially a Mannlicher he had prized—and those magnificent trophies that hung over his fireplace.

Red Chills, his right pants leg still smoldering, dragged himself into the timber and looked back just in time to see—outlined against the still-burning house—the two big creatures still in pursuit of him. They had spotted him earlier and seemed doggedly intent on chasing him down.

Hell! He was in the timber now—*his* element. And he considered himself just as dangerous as these—whatever the hell they were—any day of the week. The branches plucked at his body, tearing his shirt and britches as he crashed through the underbrush. The trees overhead shut out any light from the sky, had there been any moon capable of breaking through this damned overcast. Everything was wet, every leaf and every branch, and showered him continuously as he plunged through the thick brush. He had been forced to fling off his fur vest when it had caught fire, and he missed it sorely. It had come from the biggest goddamn grizzly he had ever seen, let alone killed.

He paused when he reached a small clearing to listen for his pursuers. At first he could hear nothing, and that surprised him, for he was sure they were still after him. Yes. The bastards were out there, all right. There was no way he could mistake that smell. It reminded him of an old mountain-man friend of his who had taken to sleeping in a cave with a black bear—and worse.

Then he saw their shadows through the trees as they neared the clearing, and smiled. It had been his intention to lure the bastards away from their brothers before making his move. He turned about and moved off through the timber, gliding along as swiftly and silently as a man his size was capable of moving.

Two hours later, topping a wooded ridge, Red looked back the way he had come, swung his shotgun around, and waited. He had already checked his load before he reached the ridge. By this time his two pursuers were strung out enough so that there were at least a couple of minutes between them. He saw the nearest one break out of a wooded copse just below the ridge, glance up, then, on silent feet, begin to climb the slope.

Son of a bitch, Red muttered. Come and get it. I'm waiting, you bastard.

In order to savor his kill, Red waited until the aborigine reached the crest of the ridge before squeezing both triggers. The shotgun misfired, tearing the breech apart in an explosion that ripped the shotgun out of his hands. Red felt the claws of metal slicing his cheek, but his eyes, though they smarted from the acrid smoke, had not been injured. Staggering back, he kept his feet and glanced at his pursuer. There was a gaping hole in his furry chest, and he was weaving slightly.

But he was not down.

One load of buckshot must have gone on its way, then. But one load was not enough for these fellows, evidently. Red pulled his long knife out of its sheath and rushed the bastard. The ugly son of a bitch put out one hand to stop him, but Red simply brushed past it and plunged his blade into the big fellow's chest as far as it would go. The aborigine shuddered like a young tree taking a hard blow from an ax. Red pulled his knife free and sliced at the giant's jugular. At once a dark fountain of warm, steaming blood gouted from his throat.

Drenched, Red stepped back as his huge opponent toppled to the ground.

Red looked back down the slope. The other one was halfway up. Swiftly he unholstered his Navy Colt, walked to the edge of the ridge, took careful aim, and began firing into the approaching aborigine. The first bullets seemed to have no effect except to slow him some. But then one bullet caught the fellow in the head, and he flung his arms up and toppled backward down the slope.

Red was holstering his gun when he heard as well as felt something moving close behind him. Before he could turn, he felt an awesome, numbing blow on his left shoulder that sent him crashing to the ground. He kept his wits about him and rolled over—and kept rolling.

The aborigine he thought he had killed was still very much alive. The giant lurched after Red, the dark fountain still gouting from his neck, gripping what was left of the shotgun's barrel in one hand. As the fellow swayed murderously over Red, the barrel poised to strike, Red fired carefully up into his face. In the darkness, it appeared as if the creature's dark features simply expanded into nothingness. Red rolled over swiftly one more time as the giant collapsed to the ground, narrowly missing him.

Slowly, gingerly, Red felt his left shoulder. No doubt about it. From the feel and the sick shock of pain now coursing through that side of his body, he knew the son of a bitch had broken his shoulder.

He got up on one knee and looked over with grudging admiration at his dead assailant. Red knew he was going to have to hole up a while and nurse himself back to health before he took after that deputy marshal. And that meant he would need meat, fresh meat—and maybe another fur vest to keep him warm while he mended.

As he looked over at the ample form of the dead mountain man, he decided he had the makings of both already in front of him. Only this time he would like a fur jacket, not just a vest. He chuckled through the pain. Hell, getting that much fur should be no trouble at all. There was enough of this goddamn aborigine to outfit an elephant.

But right now he was weak and getting weaker. What he needed was fresh meat. And soon. Red put his knife between his teeth and walked painfully over to the dead Indian—or whatever the hell he was.

Late the next day, the last ore wagon gave out less than a couple of miles from the coast. Like the others, it had been driven too hard over the uneven ground, and a boulder solidly implanted in the ground smashed the wheel. Before the wagon came to rest, its axle snapped.

Those who had not been thrown free clambered out and joined the others. The enveloping darkness gave each of them a chilled feeling of dread.

They were still being followed.

"Over there," said Jed softly. "What's that moving in those trees?"

Sir Allen shaded his eyes to see better. "You've got good eyes, Jed," the man said. "They're in there, by Jove! What splendid tenacity!"

Frida, standing close beside Longarm, shuddered. "I don't think there's anything splendid about them at all," she said.

"I agree," said Longarm. "Let's get the men organized, Sir Allen. I'd like to reach the coast before dark."

"Of course," said the Englishman. "Of course."

But Longarm could tell Sir Allen would really rather have gone into that timber after still one more trophy.

Their pursuers circled around and caught up with them before they reached the coast. They were waiting in a small patch of timber through which the party would have to go if they wanted to reach the docks that serviced Sir Allen's gold shipment. Fortunately, Sir Allen spotted them before their party reached the timber.

Longarm had his shotgun and a Colt, Sir Allen his rifle. Longarm was almost out of shells, and Sir Allen had no more than a dozen rounds.

"So what do we do now?" asked Jed nervously.

"Sir Allen and I will draw their attention away from the rest of you. When we do, you take Frida and the rest of the men through that timber, and don't look back until you reach the docks."

"Got you," said Jed.

"Be careful, Longarm," said Frida.

"With those fellows, Frida, I'll be *very* careful."

"I count at least six of them," said Sir Allen. "But I am sure there are more—all around us. I can feel them."

"I can *smell* them," said Longarm. "Let's go. We'll advance straight toward them, then draw them off toward that rise over there. It should give us good, clear shots at them as they approach. I suggest, Sir Allen, that you hold your fire until you have a sure target."

"Wait until we see the whites of their eyes, is that it, Deputy—like your ancestors at Bunker Hill."

"Yeah. That's it, all right."

"After you, Deputy."

Longarm was within a hundred feet of the timber when their would-be ambushers charged out of the timber toward them. He turned swiftly and raced toward the rise, Sir Allen puffing mightily to keep up. When they reached the top of the hillock, Longarm took careful aim and fired on the nearest one, aiming low so as to be sure to cripple him, if not kill him outright.

Sir Allen began firing with cool precision. In a matter of minutes the carnage was awesome. Only a single aborigine was standing, and he seemed no longer interested in charging up the slight incline. He might have turned away and run off, if Sir Allen had not caught him in the head.

He grabbed at his shattered skull, let out a wild bellow, and charged up the incline toward them. Longarm had difficulty believing what he was seeing. Half the Indian's skull was blown away, but he made the crest in seconds, before Longarm could close up his shotgun. As the aborigine swept past him on his way to meet Sir Allen, Longarm swung at the huge figure with his shotgun.

He struck the fellow on the chest, separating the stock from the barrel, but not slowing him down in the slightest. The aborigine's charge got him to Sir Allen just as the Englishman managed to send a second round into him. But it seemed to make no difference as the two met.

Sir Allen went down with barely a sound and was almost completely buried under the amazing bulk of his infuriated attacker. But the aborigine made no more effort to punish Sir Allen. Instead, he just lay upon the Englishman without stirring an inch. Longarm rushed over and tugged at the huge form. While he worked, he heard the Englishman's plaintive wail:

"Get me out from under this!" he cried, his voice muffled.

"I'm doing the best I can," Longarm replied as he grabbed one of the shoulders of the aborigine and pulled.

The Indian rolled off finally, and as Longarm took his

first real close-up look at one of these fellows, he felt a shock. If this was an Indian, he belonged to no tribe Longarm knew of—and that was for damned sure.

He turned his attention back to Sir Allen. The man was gasping and making only a feeble attempt to get up.

"I think my ribcage is crushed, Deputy," he managed painfully.

"Here. Let me help you up."

"Thank you, Deputy."

Sir Allen was able to stand, but his face was ashen. Longarm had seen similar injuries before; it occurred to him that if the Englishman's ribs had been crushed severely enough, they might have punctured his lungs.

Still, with barely a murmur of complaint, the man kept up with Longarm as they continued on to the coast, though he did have to stop occasionally to catch his breath; by the time Longarm and Sir Allen reached the small company town that had sprung up to service Sir Allen's gold shipments, Sir Allen was coughing up blood.

Tim and Frida, along with the others, were waiting for them on the dock. Jed had one shotgun remaining. On Longarm's request, he gave it to him, along with a handful of shells. Longarm checked out the Colt he had also, then looked anxiously at Tim.

"What about the schooner?"

"I talked to a fellow in that shed over there. He says the schooner isn't due for another hour."

"It'll be pitch dark by then," Longarm observed.

"You don't think those Indians will attack us if we're out in the open like this, do you?"

"I don't know what they aim to do," replied Longarm. "All I know is, they're taking some pains to get us the hell off their island. And as far as I'm concerned, they can have it."

Beside him, Sir Allen coughed. "I am afraid, Deputy," he said, "that I heartily concur in that sentiment."

Longarm looked over at the meager collection of buildings that had sprung up alongside the dock area. The place had no name, but it could have been called, with every justification, Pembroke City. There was, of course, a saloon, and alongside it a warehouse, and beyond that a small hotel and restaurant. A blacksmith shop across from the hotel was only a one-sided shed, the livery a rope corral behind another, equally flimsy shed. The huge workhorses that Sir Allen required to haul his ore wagons were bunched up close to the shed, a huge pile of horse manure behind them.

"Have you warned the people over there?" Longarm asked Jed.

"I tried to, but I don't think they believed me. Hell, Longarm, they think of me as one of Sir Allen's miners— and that means I must have robbed a bank or shot down a lawman. They know what human garbage has been passing through this port."

"I reckon you're right. But I suspicion they might take some advice from a lawman."

"If you can prove you *are* a lawman."

"Look!" cried Frida. "The boat!"

They all turned. The running lights of a schooner could be seen, growing brighter and larger as its dark shape emerged from a fog bank.

Sir Allen began to cough. As Longarm turned to ask him how he felt, he saw a man running from the hotel toward the dock. Behind him came another man, and a moment later, what Longarm judged to be the town's blacksmith came tearing after him.

In a moment the dock was thundering with their footsteps.

"What the hell is it?" Longarm demanded of the first to reach them.

For answer, the hotel clerk pointed back at the hotel he had just left. Smoke was pulsing from a shattered rear window, and as Longarm looked closer, he saw a man jumping out of the hotel's second-story window. He must have seriously injured his leg, but he got up anyway and limped painfully toward the docks. A moment later Longarm thought he saw a huge figure looming in an alley between the buildings.

At that moment, two girls from the saloon raced out of it, screaming, and behind them came the barkeep. All three of them headed for what was now a very crowded dock.

Longarm turned back to the strait. The schooner was a good deal closer. But it would be dark before it reached the dock.

He tapped Tim and Jed on the shoulder. "Help get this schooner docked," he told them, "but don't tie any lines too tight. We may have to get out of here in one big hurry. It looks like our furry friends have reached the coast."

"What are you going to do?" asked Sir Allen. His voice was weak and ragged.

"I'm going to borrow that rifle of yours and station myself at the other end of this dock until that schooner can get us off this damned island."

"No you aren't, Deputy. I'm going with you. This is my party, after all."

Though he tried to sound enthusiastic, he was hurting too much to pull it off, but Longarm decided not to argue with the man. "All right," he said. "With your rifle and this shotgun, we should be able to hold them off."

It was completely dark by the time they stationed themselves on the beach under the pilings and got themselves set. Most of the town's inhabitants had already crowded onto the dock by that time, those who were able to make it safely to the dock, that is. Longarm heard agonized screams break out every once in a while as someone was caught by the aborigines. Meanwhile, the fire that had broken out in the rear of the hotel had swept through the rest of the building, its flaming embers spreading the fire to the other structures.

The saloon was the next to go up, and after that the warehouse. The ship's bell sounded behind them as the schooner reached the dock. At about the same time, they saw the dark forms lumbering toward them through the smoke. They moved slowly, warily, and it was not until they were within a few yards that Longarm caught the movement on his right.

He whirled and saw four of them emerging from the sea,

as slick and shiny as seals in the darkness, but twice as large, the dark water cascading off them in sheets. Longarm emptied both barrels at the quartet, and saw two of them slow down. Sir Allen was firing with a steady, metronomic regularity at those coming at them from the town. Seeing he did not have time to reload his shotgun, Longarm took out his Colt and fired as swiftly as he could thumb-cock his weapon at the two who were still moving toward them.

One of them he stopped, but only one—and his Colt was empty.

"Sir Allen!" Longarm cried.

The Englishman spun about, lifted his rifle, worked the bolt, and fired. The remaining aborigine doubled over, reached out to grab a piling, then slid down its length to the ground. Swiftly, Longarm reloaded his Colt and the shotgun.

Longarm heard Sir Allen scream. He spun about and saw the Englishman in the clutches of two more of them. They had come out of the water on the other side of the dock.

As Sir Allen's screams were abruptly and mercifully choked off, Longarm fled up the beach and raced up onto the dock. Only one of the aborigines made any effort to stop him, and Longarm slowed him with a bullet in the chest. As he raced past him onto the dock, he saw Jed hurrying toward him, a Winchester in his hand.

"I got this from the captain," Jed cried.

Longarm pulled up and looked back. To his surprise, the aborigines were not following him onto the dock. Squinting through the smoke-filled darkness, he saw them moving off in a group. In the garish light of the dancing flames, Longarm thought he saw the aborigines dragging what looked like Sir Allen's broken body between them.

Carrying their trophy, the strange tribe headed swiftly toward the dark timber. In a moment they had disappeared completely, the bodies of their fellows still littering the flame-lit ground in mute testimony to Sir Allen's marksmanship.

"It was Sir Allen they wanted," said Jed softly.

Longarm nodded grimly.

They turned then and hurried aboard the schooner. A moment later the ship—under the outlaws' control now—cast off. Longarm was leaning on a rail in the stern when the ship's sails caught the hot, cinder-laden night wind and heeled sharply over. Longarm looked back at the burning company town and found himself thinking of Sir Allen.

There was no doubt the man was more than a little mad in what he had been attempting to do; and there was no doubt that his activities were criminal and had to be stopped. Yet the scope of his audacious undertaking, his creation of the Devil's Railroad, bordered on genius.

But—more important in Longarm's eyes—in addition to genius, Sir Allen had courage, a cool, almost serene confidence under fire that at first Longarm had mistaken for foolhardiness.

And twice he had saved Longarm's life. Whether it had been out of self interest or not, that indisputable fact remained.

The burning town vanished in the mist of the strait, leaving only a glow to mark its presence. Longarm turned away from the railing. He thought he could smell hot coffee brewing in the galley. He would have preferred something stronger, but for now he would settle for that.

Anything to get the chill of death out of his bones.

Red Chills had seen the glow in the night sky and had guessed what that meant, so he kept to the south of the company town as he worked his way through the timber toward the coast. His recently acquired pelt he wore thrown over his shoulders like a rough fur cape. He had bound his broken shoulder tightly with strips torn from his shirt, then used his belt as a sling. Most painful to him at the moment were the deep, disfiguring cuts on his face from the fragments of the shotgun's bursting breech. He had dug out any jagged pieces of metal and cleaned the wounds with mountain water, but his face had been burned raw by the exploding powder and felt like a tight, constricting mask.

He was tough, however, and for him the pain was manageable; in fact, in a way he welcomed it, since it added fuel to his desire to avenge himself on that meddlesome deptuy marshal.

So he felt reasonably cheerful as he stepped out of the timber into a surprisingly bright morning and saw the two Indians on the beach below, loading their canoe for a day's fishing. Chills recognized them at once as Nootkas, but they were not of the nobility, judging by the modest size of their fishing canoe.

Without hesitation, he started down the rocks that led to the beach, moving carefully, deliberately because of his shoulder. He had not gone far when the two Indians discovered him. At first they simply watched him curiously, but when he reached the beach and started across the sand, and they got a whiff of him, their calm expression changed with comical speed.

They let out a cry and bolted. Chills pulled up and roared with laughter. They had smelled his pelt, he realized. All the coast Indians, he knew—the Chilkat, the Kwakiutl, the Coast Salish—were terrified of that giant, hairy tribe that lived in the island's interior.

And now they would be terrified of him as well. He did not bother to take any precautions as he waded out into the shallow water, pushed the Nootkas' canoe out into the deeper water, then climbed clumsily into it. Reaching for the paddle, he realized he would have difficulty making it across the strait to the mainland with only one good arm, but he was in no hurry.

He knew where that deputy had started from—a town in Idaho it was, a place called Ridge Town, where the local and federal law had conspired to let that son of a bitch pull off a fake robbery. The Englishman had found out what had happened, and then had explained it all to Red. When he had finished with his explanation, he had laughed as if it were all a big joke.

But it wasn't any joke to Red Chills. Good friends of his were dead now, and too many of them at the hands of this deputy. And the Englishman's railroad was finished, leaving Red with nothing to show for this last trip but a bag full of phony bills.

It wasn't funny at all.

As he paddled clumsily out into the deeper water, he glanced back and saw the Nootkas lining the ridge along the shore. He lifted his paddle out of the water and waved it at them. Almost to a man, the Indians shrank back out of sight.

Chuckling meanly, Red turned back around and began digging into the heavy swells.

Chapter 12

"All you need, Longarm," Frida said, "is just a little more wax, and it will look just fine."

"That's right," said Tim.

Longarm peered at his mustache a moment longer, then stepped away from the broken mirror and nodded in agreement. He had settled up with the remains of Sir Allen's miners in Squamish and sent them—along with a very eager Jed—on their way to South America in Sir Allen's schooner, a very unhappy captain serving as their unwilling navigator and a pretty badly torn up Bill Robinson making do as first mate.

In the month since, while the three of them made their way back to Idaho, Longarm had been attempting to grow back his longhorn mustache. Now, back in the cabin where he had first transformed himself into Wolf Caulder, he surveyed the results and was grudgingly satisfied. Just a little more wax and the mustache would be standing up as good as new.

Now he turned away from the mirror and requested that Frida and her brother wait outside while he changed. Grinning at Longarm's apparent shyness, they left the ramshackle cabin together.

Longarm went to the cot, pushed it aside, knelt on the floor, and pried up the loose floorboards under which he had left his own familiar clothing and weaponry. Everything was as he had left it. He took his tobacco-brown Stetson from the hole, dusted it off lovingly, and propped it on his head while he lifted out the carpetbag that contained the rest of his clothing, then removed the bundle of oil-soaked rags that held his Colt, his derringer, and his watch.

Dressing swiftly, he breathed a comfortable sigh at the feeling of normalcy that his accustomed garb gave him. He then strapped on his waxed and heat-hardened cross-draw holster, adjusted it on his hips, and opened the package that contained his guns and watch.

He examined both weapons carefully, wiping off any excess oil with a clean rag, then loaded them, checking each round of .44-40 ammunition for wear, and making sure no oil had seeped in around the primer caps.

He dropped the Colt into its holster and drew it a few times, and nodded in satisfaction. This was more like it.

Next he wound his watch and set it, then attached the derringer to the special clip at the other end of the gold-washed watch chain. He dropped the watch into his left-hand vest pocket, and the derringer into the right-hand pocket, letting the chain drape elegantly across his vest front.

Adjusting the Stetson so it sat straight on his head, he walked toward the cabin door and opened it.

As he stepped out into the sunshine, Frida turned and looked at him, and her mouth dropped open. Tim smiled widely, obviously impressed. Longarm knew then that his transformation was complete; he was back in uniform again.

He walked to his horse, a big, broad-chested dun, and mounted up, saying, "We've spent enough time here. Let's start riding. I'd like to reach Ridge Town by nightfall."

As they rode out, Tim urged his mount closer to Longarm's. Longarm could see at once that Tim was still worried. "You sure this is the right thing for me to do, Longarm?"

"It is, unless you want to spend the rest of your life as a fugitive."

"But the sheriff in this county's got it in for me. It doesn't matter what your boss wired you in Squamish, Sheriff Dinwiddee doesn't have to go along."

"No he don't, and that's a fact. But you let me talk to him. I'm sure Marshal Vail has already wired him—and federal marshals have some clout with these local politicians, don't forget."

"I hope you're right."

"Just let Longarm try," said Frida. "It can't hurt to let him try."

Tim looked at Frida and smiled. "Sure, Sis. You got a point there, and I know it. Besides, I don't want you traipsing all over hell and beyond looking for me anymore."

Tim looked back at Longarm.

"Let's go, Longarm. I'm ready."

Longarm spurred his horse gently down the slope as Tim and Frida followed. He had sounded confident enough just now, but the difficulty was that he didn't feel nearly as confident as he had sounded. Longarm had wired Billy Vail the good news about the end of the Devil's Railroad as soon as he'd reached Squamish and finished settling matters with that first mate.

But after that, there had been a series of wires exchanged between Longarm and Billy Vail, dealing with the disposition of Tim Terrill's case. It was Longarm's contention that Tim had been instrumental in helping a deputy U. S. marshal bring a federal case to a successful conclusion. At the very least, Tim should be given a pardon. If that was not possible, Longarm wanted Sheriff Dinwiddee to recall the escaped-fugitive warrants he had issued after Tim's escape.

An exasperated Billy Vail had sent Longarm one final telegram, telling him he would back Longarm's play with

Sheriff Dinwiddee, but Longarm would have to deal with the sheriff himself.

And that was how matters stood at the moment. What Longarm wanted to know now was how Sheriff Dinwiddee had taken that lesson in sharpshooting Longarm had given him when he was masquerading as Wolf Caulder. He hoped the sheriff had a good sense of humor.

Red Chills swore bitterly. It was sundown, and two of the riders coming in from the Bitterroots he recognized well enough, no matter how poor the light. Tim and his sister. But the third rider wasn't the deputy. So where the hell was he?

Sitting up in his hotel window, back far enough behind the curtains to be invisible from the street, he was ready to call down for another whiskey, when he took a second look at that gent with Tim and his sister.

The three of them had dismounted in front of Dinwiddee's office, and as the tall gent stepped up onto the board-walk, Chills slapped his thigh in sudden, belated recognition. That long-legged stride was a dead giveaway. It was the deputy, sure enough! Only now he was sporting a fancy mustache, a flat-crowned brown Stetson, and slick wool duds.

A pleased smile on his face, Red watched the three enter the sheriff's office, then got to his feet.

"Why, dammit, Longarm!" Sheriff Dinwiddee roared. "You near killed me and two of my deputies. And when you took off Slim Donner's hat with that last shot, he swore off riding with me or any other posse. God blast it to hellfire, man, you made me shit in my britches!" He glanced quickly at Frida. "Excuse me, ma'am."

"That's all right, Sheriff," she said, her voice small and worried.

"Just tryin' to make it look good, Dinwiddee. You know that."

"*I* knew what you was tryin' to do. But no one else did, and you didn't have to make it look *that* good, did you?"

"I reckon I let myself get carried away some. But it ain't me that's got to be discussed, Sheriff. It's this boy here— a brave young man who helped me crack that Devil's Railroad case."

Sheriff Dinwiddee looked at Tim. The sheriff was a big man who had, in the past four or five years, turned to suet in the oddest way. It was as if he had not become fat, but simply lumpy—all over. His belly. His arms. His face. "You've done been convicted of murder, Tim," the sheriff said, not unkindly. "You've got to pay the price for that crime. It won't do you no good to have this soft-hearted U. S. deputy come in here to speak for you. I'm sorry, boy, but the law's the law, and there ain't no way a man can change that. You been tried and you been convicted. And that's the end of it."

"Hell, Dinwiddee," said Longarm. "You know that ain't true. You mean to tell me you ain't heard some talk hereabouts, saying that maybe Tim wasn't the one that killed that fellow?"

"Well, sure. I heard something."

"You heard this kid here got suckered so someone else could walk away—someone mighty important in these parts. Now you've heard that, ain't you?"

Dinwiddee began to sweat. "Now, dammit, Longarm. That ain't nothin' but talk, and you know it."

"What ain't talk, Dinwiddee, is the service this man— and his sister—provided for the federal government. That deputy who was killed? He had powerful friends in Washington. They'll sure as hell want to know what happened to the young man who helped break that ring."

"Now hold it just a doggone minute, Longarm. You ain't got no cause to go telling tales on me to Washington. That ain't fair."

"You willing to palaver some more on this?"

The man hesitated. "Well," he said, glancing uncertainly toward Tim and his sister. "There ain't no crime in talking. But I ain't promisin' nothin', you understand."

"How about the saloon next to the First National Bank?" Longarm asked, grinning suddenly.

With a weary shrug, Sheriff Dinwiddee pushed himself out of his chair and lifted his hat down off a hook on the wall. Leading the way out of his office, he said, "I'm tellin' you again. I ain't promisin' a thing."

It was almost midnight, and a very drunk Sheriff Dinwiddee was shaking his head doggedly while he hung on to his half-full shot glass. He was close to tears, but he was not weakening on the fundamentals.

Though he saw clearly now the gross injustice that had been visited upon Tim, he simply could not get himself to withdraw his warrants—even on the condition that Tim leave Idaho Territory and never return again to disturb its tranquil ways.

Tim looked dispiritedly over at Longarm and smiled wanly. "That's all right, Longarm," he said. "You've done your best. I'll just have to ride out of here a fugitive."

"No," said Dinwiddee, blinking his eyes to clear them, then drawing his sixgun and pointing it across the table at Tim. "You are my prisoner. You ain't riding off nowhere. You're under arrest."

Both Tim and Longarm were shocked into silence.

It was Frida who broke it.

"Longarm!" she cried. "That smell!"

The saloon was almost completely deserted by this time. Longarm looked swiftly around him. He had caught the stench at almost the same time as Frida. It was getting more powerful by the minute and seemed to be coming from the rear of the saloon.

Dinwiddee began to laugh. "It's that mountain man! Ain't it awful? Smells worse'n a manure pile in spring. MacPherson's been tryin' to get the big filthy bastard out of his hotel for the past week."

Turning, Dinwiddee pointed to the rear of the saloon. Red Chills stepped into view, a gleaming sixgun in his hand and murder in his eyes. He was wearing a long, matted fur overcoat—the source of his powerful advertisement.

"Hey, Red!" Dinwiddee cried, his voice slurred from the alcohol he had consumed. "You can come in here for that drink now. Like I said, it's late and the place is pretty near empty. But put away that damn shootin' iron, or I'll have to arrest you for disorderly conduct."

The sheriff belched.

Longarm went for his Colt. Chills began firing just as Tim leaped to his feet and shoved the sheriff out of the line of fire. The sheriff dropped his sixgun and went over backward as the first round hit the top of the table and ricocheted past Longarm's right temple. The second round caught Tim's thigh and flung him sprawling across the table. His tumbling body struck Longarm's gun hand just as Longarm was raising it to return the fire. Longarm was sent sprawling backwards, the table going over with him.

As Tim and Longarm crouched behind the table, Chills continued to fire until his gun was empty, then vanished out the saloon's back door. Dazed but unhurt, Longarm jumped to his feet and looked down at Tim. Frida was already at her brother's side, fighting back tears as she yanked down his britches to examine his thigh wound. It was bleeding profusely, and she was desperate to stem the flow of blood.

"Use the tablecloth!" cried a suddenly very sober Sheriff Dinwiddee. "Tie it around his leg."

At once, Frida snatched up the red-checked tablecloth and began to rip it into narrow strips. Assuming that Tim would be well taken care of, Longarm raced out the rear door after Red Chills. He found it pitch black behind the saloon, but he was not worried—not as long as he had his sense of smell.

Testing the wind like a dog on the scent of game, he headed north. Then, still following his nose, he turned down another alley, this one leading past the hotel. He was hurrying along, gun drawn, bent over so as not to give Red a bigger than necessary target, when Red's stench became overpowering on his right. Longarm whirled, bringing his sixgun up—but he was too late.

A sawed-off porch beam came down hard on the side of his head, slashing at his ear and knocking him back against an outhouse with such force that the little shack nearly rocked off its foundation. Slumping dazedly to the ground,

161

Longarm shook his head in an effort to clear it. He was dimly aware that he had dropped his Colt, and began to feel frantically about on the ground for it.

Red stepped down off the hotel's back porch and approached. "Hello, you son of a bitch," Chills said, kicking Longarm's sixgun down the alley. "Now it's my turn."

Red's foot lashed out, catching Longarm under the ribs and flipping him over. Longarm tried to get up, but another well-aimed boot caught him in the groin. The pain was so intense he almost lost consciousness. Red hunkered down beside him, grabbed his hair with a massive fist, and yanked his head up so he could talk to him.

"Been waitin' for you," Chills told Longarm. "Got a bum shoulder or I would of caught up to you sooner. Almost missed you in them new duds and that fine mustache." He laughed and spat in Longarm's face. "Got any more surprises?"

Longarm fired both barrels of his derringer into the man's stomach.

"The way I see it," said Longarm, "Tim saved both our lives. But there ain't no question about it, Sheriff. That first bullet of Red's—the one that sliced the tabletop—would've caught you in the head if Tim hadn't knocked you on your ass when he did."

It was the following morning, and Longarm and the sheriff were talking over breakfast in the hotel dining room. Longarm's side and groin were tender, but the breakfast had been a good one, and he had found a place that sold his favorite cheroots. He had just lit one a minute before.

Tim was upstairs, resting peacefully, with Frida by his side. The doctor had come and gone, predicting a long and healthy life for Tim if he could escape any more bad luck. And that was precisely what Longarm was attempting to accomplish for the young man.

"Well, I was too drunk to remember it all that clear," said Dinwiddee. "But I guess you're right, at that. Tim wouldn't have got shot if he'd jumped the other way, out of the line of fire."

Longarm sat back and eyed the sheriff. "You just said it. And you're right. Now are you going to send such a lad to prison? Were those actions of his the actions of a cowardly murderer?"

"Damn it, Longarm?"

"Answer me, Sheriff. And don't make me throw up when you do."

The big man sighed. "All right. I'll go along with Billy Vail, and I'll recall them warrants. But Tim'll have to find a different home than Idaho Territory. After all, I got to live here, and there's factions I got to consider."

"I understand, Sheriff."

Longarm reached across the table and shook the man's hand on it.

Tim was waiting for him in the Hotel Windsor's lobby when Longarm entered two weeks later. Though Tim and his sister had arrived in Denver the night before, it was obvious to Longarm that Tim was still dazzled by the hotel's gleaming lobby and the plush accommodations.

Shaking Tim's hand, Longarm asked, "How's the leg?"

"Almost as good as new—except when I try to ride, or get up too quickly."

"That should go soon enough. Did Frida enjoy her trip?"

"She sure did. Listen, Longarm, I want you to know how much I appreciate what you and that Marshal Vail—"

Longarm stopped him with a wave and a smile. "You don't need to thank me. *I'm* the one to thank *you*. Ready?"

"Yes, sir. I'm ready."

The two men walked into the bar and found a table to the rear. They ordered drinks and were joined not long after by a man whom Longarm introduced as Mr. Paul Welling. At once he and Tim got down to business. The two got on fine together. Welling had the finances, and Tim had the knowledge Welling needed, the knowledge that could tell Welling not only where Sir Allen's gold mine was, but also how they could move into the island's interior and out again with enough gold ore to make the trip worthwhile—and before any strange inhabitants of the region gathered themselves once again to throw them out.

It was a risky venture, but there would be a sizable stake in it for Tim—and a chance to put all his bad luck behind him.

As Tim and Welling shook hands, Longarm decided he'd done all he could. He excused himself and left the two as they began making plans. He walked into the lobby and was about to approach the front desk to find out Frida's room number when he heard his name called—softly, but urgently.

He turned and saw Frida on the wide staircase. She was not wearing jeans or a man's shirt, but a long, sweeping, brown corduroy dress that set off beautifully her dark eyes and auburn curls. There was white lace at her throat. Her hair was swept back in the latest fashion. In the few short weeks that had passed since he had said goodbye to her in Ridge Town, she seemed to have been transformed into a creature far lovelier than he would have imagined possible.

As she swept off the stairs and hurried to his side, however, he saw that her eyes held the same impudent fire in them. It was the old warm Frida in a new, lovelier package.

She thrust her arm through his.

"I just came down to find you," she said. "And now that I have, we're going right back upstairs—together."

He saw no reason to argue with her.

SPECIAL PREVIEW

Here are the opening scenes
from

LONGARM IN SILVER CITY

fortieth novel in the bold
LONGARM series from Jove

Chapter 1

Longarm sniffed trouble like a steer catching the scent of water in the middle of alkali flats.

What's eatin' at me? he inquired savagely, behind that polite mask of his face where no one could hear and become unduly alarmed at some hatchet-faced jasper talking to himself.

All he knew was that some unwanted embroilment lurked just up the trail. He knew this, even when he had nothing to go on except instinct. And he wasn't about to start mistrusting his instincts; they'd kept him alive down a lot of backtrails.

He scowled at the backs of his callused hands. What the contention might be and how far along the trace, he couldn't be sure, but like that thirsty steer sniffing the air, he prickled with the dead-certain feeling that it was there, waiting.

His first inkling of wrong struck him when his through-coach going south stopped at Socorro in the blaze of a hot, dry morning. Nothing unusual in a scheduled stop, but the driver poked his bewhiskered face in the tonneau window and made it all as odd as hell.

"You're gettin' off here, Mr. Long." The driver's hoarse voice was a bellow, even when pitched in a friendly and conversational tone.

Something stirred deep inside Longarm's belly, that faint fluttering of alarm. "Why?"

The driver grinned at him, withdrew, and swung up on the iron rungs. Longarm saw his new hard-leather, government-issue bag untied from the baggage-stacked roofing and thrown casually into the gray dirt outside the adobe way station.

"What the hell," Longarm protested. "I might have liquor in there."

The bearded driver just smiled at him and shrugged. "Hope so, Mr. Long. You'll plumb need it where you're goin'."

The driver turned away as Longarm stepped down from the battered old stagecoach. He caught the big man's arm lightly, but detained him firmly. "How come you're puttin' me off here? I got a through ticket."

"Yep." The man nodded his head. "All the way to Silver City."

"Do I have to tell you this is Socorro?"

"Reckoned it to be." The driver nodded his head again and spat a brown glob of tobacco juice into the dirt between them. "You're goin' on to Silver City. But we ain't headed that way, mister. We follow the old Spanish Trail 'longside the Rio Grandy, south to Las Cruces." He bobbed his battered Stetson toward a gleaming coach parked carefully in the shade of a cottonwood. "That there is your coach. You'll travel to hell in style, anyhow. Come to think of it, that there coach do resemble a hearse, now don't it?"

He slapped his fat leg and walked away laughing.

Carrying his dust-smeared bag, Longarm limped over to the stylish coach. His gimpy walk resulted from no bodily injury except the total exhaustion of an eternal stagecoach ride southwest from Denver, plus the cramped position of his long legs in the narrow space between facing seats designed for midgets. Also, an ill-healed bulletwound nagged at the fringes of his consciousness. One thing about a gun wound: it plain hurt, going in and coming out. And even when it cured up and scarred over, it twinged irregularly, just to remind you.

The driver was right, this carriage did look like one of those stylish hearses used in Denver when some political bigwig, silver mine operator, or first-family member kicked off.

He exhaled, surveying the carriage. It boasted narrow, steel-rimmed wheels. Leaf-spring thoroughbraces were slung to absorb some of the roadshock. No doubt, this vehicle was the finest example of luxury-equipage craft. Its interior was upholstered in dark blue velvet; facing seats, with ample knee room, were deeply padded and plush. Framed glass windows slid up and down on cord straps in the door, for comfort in any kind of weather.

The graceful body, of finest hand-rubbed mahogany, shone until he could glimpse his travel-weary reflection in its burnished depths. It was like looking at himself in a dark mirror.

Longarm was none too elated or reassured by what he saw. His gray flannel shirt bore long, heavy sweat streaks. In the close, breathless heat of that stagecoach across the barren white New Mexico desert, he was beginning to smell old and used.

He admitted he still looked lean and hard enough to cut the mustard—muscular, with shoulders that strained the fabric of his frock coat. Time, pitiless suns, and burning snows had wind-cured his rawboned face to a saddle-leather brown. No softness was exposed in the gunmetal blue of his sun-faded eyes, either. They remained young, watchful, and wary. He watched his reflection touch at its neatly waxed longhorn mustache, proud and flaring between a sharp-hewn nose and a taut-lipped mouth. His snuff-brown Stetson, its crown telescoped in the Colorado fashion, tilted low over his dark brows, positioned carefully, slightly forward, cavalry-style, to shade and almost conceal his eyes.

169

He sighed and turned away. When a man began to go to fat in his business, it was time to rack the guns. Trouble moved fast, and you had to be ready—to run it down or, if need be, to outrun it for a second chance another day.

He smiled grimly, chewing at his unlit two-for-a-nickel cheroot. Ever since he'd run away from his home in West-by-God-Virginia to ride in the big war, he'd been dealing with trouble, one way or another.

He shook his head, sweating in the dead heat and silence of the little trail town. In all those years, he'd never become too damned enamored of trouble, either. He could take it or leave it.

"Por favor! Por favor! Cuidado, Señor!"

Three hostlers, half-running, led a team of harnessed horses around the adobe building and hitched them to the coach. Longarm sagged in the shade of the dust-hung, leaf-sagging cottonwood, waiting.

The stablehands argued dispassionately but intensely in broken English about some disagreement from the previous night over a town girl named Lupe. They did not glance again toward Longarm.

When the horses were hitched in place and the lines carefully wrapped and waiting around the whipstock on the carriage boot, the three men plodded back around the building in the blazing sun, still arguing desultorily.

"Howdy, friend. You the fare going to Silver City on this coach with us?"

Longarm turned, nodding. This medium-tall man was impressive looking, and one recognized him on sight as *un hombre rico*, a man of untold affluence, power, position, and unquestioned authority, all of which he wore as easily as he sported the tailored suit of finest brown worsted, impeccable matching Stetson flat-crown, and hand-tooled, Mexican-ornamented brown boots with silver tips. His hands were pinkly scrubbed, the nails recently manicured and buffed. But he didn't look like a fop or a dandy. He looked like a man who had earned every dollar of his considerable wealth one at a time, with no help from anybody. Those hands had once borne scars and calluses, even if time had healed and softened them, and those smiling blue eyes carried dark secrets in their depths.

This was a world-smart man, outgoing, free-handed, and congenial, with the bluff, hearty openness of the Westerner; but he was wary and on guard at the same time.

"This crate is mine," the man said. He drew his palm along its polished beauty, then thrust out his hand. Longarm shook it, finding the grip strong, and unrelenting. "What I do is, I let the stage people use it for public conveyance whenever I travel out of Silver City. Hate fiercely to ride anywhere alone, you know. I figure man's naturally a socializing animal. By the way, the name's W. W. Meriman. Might be you've heard of me."

Longarm smiled and nodded at the modest suggestion. He knew W. W. Meriman, all right. The name Meriman was big even in Denver, the center of the silver market. Among other things, Meriman owned silver mines, smelters, and land all through Grant County. "I've heard," he said.

Meriman grinned. "What's your handle, friend?"

"Custis Long."

Meriman peered up at him, still grinning. "You're a big 'un, ain't you? Six-two? Six-three? Something like that?"

"Something like that. Being a whole foot longer than the average male ain't all that great. Beds ain't long enough. Some doors ain't tall enough. And you can't even hide in crowds."

"Do a lot of hiding, do you?"

Longarm grinned. "If you're asking what my trade is, I'm a lawman."

"Son of a gun. Might have suspected as much. I reckon when you speak, people listen, huh?"

"That's one of the things I've heard about *you*."

Meriman laughed. "That's my money people listen to. You got enough money, folks bow and scrape to you no matter what kind of turd you might be personally."

Longarm shrugged. "A man has enough money, he can afford to be a turd."

"I reckon." Meriman shook his head, considering it all.

171

"But you know, I never set out to pile up a lot of money in banks. For what? For somebody to fight over when I'm dead? Hell, making money was a sideline for me. A kind of fringe benefit. When I massed up too much, I'd run out and try to spend it off—on the usual trinkets, straight whiskey, crooked cards, and laughing women. Always have loved myself a laughing woman. But it seemed like I couldn't spend it fast enough, and it kept sticking in my accounts, or coming back double every dime I spent. You fool around with mining long enough—in the right place and at the right time—and that's liable to happen.

"Hell, I contracted the prospecting fever when I was a pecker-sized kid. I left home with a few greenbacks that nobody wanted to take in them days—hell, I never could get a Mexican to accept paper money. *Nada. Nada.* They wanted gold or silver.

"Anyhow, I pitched in with some footloose hombres who owned a mule team. I was hired to punch along the lead mule. That's all right until you try to ford a stream. You ever forded a creek with a donkey or a mule?"

"A few times."

"Mighty peculiar thing I learned from that mule. No matter how deep or swift a creek was, them danged animals always stopped to crap right in the middle of it, and all hell couldn't move them until they dumped their load and got ready to move on. By then, bedding was usually soaked through, and any flour would be wet and useless.

"Anyhow, first pay strike I ever made was in Elizabeth Town. It was on Ute Creek and panned out pretty good. Placer mining was new to me, but it wasn't long before I knew how to detect the color in a pan. We panned old riverbeds and sifted through diggings. Came on some bedrock and hit some mean pay streaks. First deposits I ever worked were shallow, and I got them out with a pick and shovel. Saw a lot of hydraulic-pressure mining, but that looked like too much work for a young kid.

"I liked working with them sluice boxes. Some of them were three or four hundred feet long. We set up a fair outfit—long-tom, sluice box, and flume. The long-tom looked like a coffin set up on a trestle and tipped toward the sluice box.

"Those old sluice boxes we used to build of raw, rough lumber, like a trough with both ends open. Slats or riffles were laid crosswise in the bottom of the sluice. The riffles caught the free metal. We learned all the tricks. Used mercury to help catch the gold, 'cause gold is drawn to quicksilver, you know. When quicksilver was used, you ended up with a mess of metal, so you had to clean up once a week or so.

"We learned to separate the gold from quicksilver or any other foreign metals. This was called cupelling. The metal was put in a porous bone-ash cup, set in a furnace, and exposed to a blast of air. Oxidized metal dropped into the pores of the cup, whilst the mercury was vaporized and caught in the chimney and used again. Only pure gold was left in the cupel.

"I soon got so I could tell a rich pay streak from a poor one. I took to mining like a pig takes to warm mud. But I got itchy feet, and before long I sold out my half of a good claim and headed south with a horse and pack mule. I traveled light—a few groceries, Arbuckle coffee, slab of salt bacon, and a sack of flour that I soon learned to carry on my head when we crossed creeks.

"Well, hell, I ended up down in the Sierra Diablo mountain ranges. That's what we called it, them days. Devil Mountains. Folks call it the Black Range now.

"I was young and full of vinegar and thought I knew all there was to know about mining—and I did know placer mining pretty fair—but down in the Black Range country, you didn't get much gold and damned little silver that easy. You blasted it out of hard rock down here, or you didn't get it at all."

A tall, rail-thin man in Levi's, scuffed boots, and a denim jacket sauntered out of the adobe hut and crossed the sun-baked yard toward the shade of the cottonwood. He picked at his teeth with a whittled pine stick and sucked air through his cavities. He bowed his head and spoke with a lot of respect. "We ought to be headin' out soon, Mr. Meriman.

Them other folks have et and all."

"Ready any time you are, Tom-Tom," Meriman said. He nodded toward Longarm. "This here is lawman Custis Long. Tom-Tom's one hell of a driver, Mr. Long. Been with me 'most twelve years now—and 'cept for almost gettin' our scalps lifted by Victorio's Chiricahua Apaches a few times, he's done right well."

Tom-Tom bobbed his head toward Longarm. "You a U. S. marshal, huh?"

Longarm winced slightly. Nobody had said who he worked for. That nagging sense of uneasiness buzzed around him again, as pesky as a deerfly.

He said nothing. Tom-Tom placed his bag on the roof baggage rack, then stacked W. W. Meriman's three calf-leather bags atop it. Tom-Tom was still hanging on the side rungs when a big voice, used to making itself heard in range gales, called from the door of the stage stop: "Stay up there, Tom-Tom. Got a couple valises for you."

Two small Mexican boys ran with the suitcases and handed them up to Tom-Tom, squinting against the sun. The aging man tossed each of them a silver coin and the boys backed away, grinning.

"Doesn't take much to make a Mexican kid happy, does it?" he said. Then his eyes widened. "Well, damn my soul! Longarm! Why, I haven't seen you since you visited us in Lincoln County that time. Nobody killed you off yet, huh?"

"Not yet, Mr. Chisum."

John Chisum wrung Longarm's hand. He said, "What in hell are you doing down this way?"

Something in Chisum's tone convinced Longarm that his business in Silver City, were he to explain it to the millionaire rancher, would be less than a surprise. So far, three out of three had known he was in the area, and very likely they knew why.

"They send me around to stir up trouble when there isn't any, Mr. Chisum," Longarm said.

Something flickered across Chisum's eyes, but he smiled and the big voice boomed. "You've already made the acquaintance of W. W. Meriman, huh? Did he tell you about his trip to New York City yet?"

174

"Not yet."

Meriman smiled and Chisum laughed aloud. "You're going to think I'm lying, Longarm. You've got to know W. W. Meriman like I do to believe it. He has the reputation for plain demolishing whole saloons when he gets likkered up enough. Word came back that he destroyed several saloons right on Broadway. He made a speech on the corner of Forty-second and Broadway, in front of one of the saloons he personally put out of business temporarily. You know what he told those good people of New York? He told them that they lived too far from Silver City ever to amount to anything!"

W. W. Meriman smiled in a modest way. "It seemed no more than a reasonable statement of fact to me," he said.

John Chisum climbed into the coach and sat down, breathing heavily. Age was an enemy the old cattleman couldn't conquer.

Longarm watched Chisum settle in the far corner of the tonneau, facing forward. It was as if this were the best seat, reserved for the Lincoln County stockman.

Watching the rancher, Longarm decided that Chisum hadn't changed much. He was a spare man, big-boned, his skin the color and texture of old, chewed leather. He wore boots as scuffed and broken as Tom-Tom's, with the bottoms of his frayed and faded Levi's tucked inside. His long, gaunt face narrowed to a jutting jaw. His hawk nose reared prominently, his graying brows were thick, his salt-and-pepper mustache full and bushy. The dark, piercing eyes regarded Longarm with something like suspicion.

"You'll have to get down to my place for a visit again soon, Marshal," he said.

"I sure will if I have time, sir."

"Nobody will try to shoot you this time," Chisum said, laughing.

Longarm was saved from answering by the arrival of the next passenger.

This gentleman was distinguished looking, with a pink, steak-fed face, and pale eyes under thick brows. In his early forties, he was not in the same financial class with Meriman or Chisum. His black suit and store-bought, high-topped black shoes were reasonably priced and advertised that the man lived on a government salary, and Longarm knew this wasn't easy.

"Morning, Judge McLoomis," W. W. Meriman said. His voice was hearty, though his blue eyes didn't manage to smile. "Good to have you along."

"Always a rare pleasure to be in your company, sir," Judge McLoomis said. He nodded his head, smiling, and removed his derby hat. His high forehead rose to prematurely gray hair, brushed back in waves, collar-length. "You're always the life of any gathering, W. W."

"A born politician," Meriman said to Longarm. "You'll seldom hear Judge Lynch McLoomis say a wrong thing, or an unpolitic thing, or an unpopular thing. Sometimes what he says don't make sense, but—"

"Maybe it just doesn't make sense to those who don't want to understand, W. W.," Judge McLoomis said with a mildly wry smile. He glanced at Longarm and extended his hand, with something like a look of relief flooding his florid face. "You're the federal marshal, eh? I wondered how long it would be before they sent one of you fellows down here."

Longarm shook the judge's hand, but he was not about to play stupid for them. He said, "Good to meet you, Judge. But I still don't understand. I came on the quiet, ahead of time. What I'd like to know is, how'd every one of you people—including Tom-Tom the driver—know who I am, and what I'm doing here?"

Judge Lynch McLoomis's pink face flushed. He glanced around, confused. Inside the coach, John Chisum laughed. "Looks like Judge Lynch McLoomis is human after all, doesn't it? He can put his foot in his mouth just like any of us ordinary folks."

Judge McLoomis sighed and faced Longarm. He tried to smile, without a great deal of success. "We've all just come back from the territorial legislative session in Santa Fe, Mr. Long. All the talk up there was about the trouble festering and ready to burst in Silver City, and what the federal government was going to do about it when we

176

couldn't get action from the army, the legislature, or Governor Wallace."

"I hope you fellows aren't barking up the wrong tree," Longarm said. "I'm here on a plain, simple mission."

"They all are," Chisum said. "I warn you, boy. Nothing is as simple as it seems in Silver City these days."

"Except maybe some of the people," Judge McLoomis said. "Everybody wants to talk, and nobody wants to listen. As I've said a dozen times, there are federal laws, and once you break them, you can count on Uncle Sam sending somebody in."

Nobody bothered to answer Judge McLoomis. Neither Chisum nor Meriman seemed overly impressed by the magistrate, though that in itself seemed odd, since Longarm knew Chisum and Meriman were on sides irreconcilably opposed to one another.

Meriman spoke under his breath. "Well, we can get it on the road now. Here comes ol' Chili Con Carne and his slutty daughter." His voice rose. "Get the Don's baggage aboard, Tom-Tom, and let's head for home."

Longarm watched the Spanish grandee and his daughter cross the sunstruck yard, and caught his breath.

Here were more of the principals in the fight down at Silver City. Four deadly enemies and the presiding judge. Looked as if it ought to be a great trip, these people locked together in a hot stagecoach.

The grandee and his daughter were two beautiful people. The Don carried his huge sombrero, embroidered with bands of real silver and nugget gold, as were his other vestments, from his beige jacket of doeskin to the buckles on his fine tan *zapatos*.

He was a big man, with silver hair that caught and reflected the sunlight. His face was the color and texture of old gold, his black eyes large and commanding. His features were sharply hewn; he had the look of the tenth-generation aristocrat. The most striking thing about him, though, was his graceful, pantherlike stride. He seeed to move effortlessly, gliding across the sun-braised ground as if he owned it and this whole corner of the universe.

But the man's daughter was the one who really caught Longarm's eye. She moved as if dancing to unseen marimbas. In her lace mantilla and ankle-length muslin walking dress of bright Spanish print, she gathered all light and air and fire. There was a radiance about her, from her rich black hair caught with combs, to her silver-tipped slippers winking as she glided beside her distinguished parent.

Her brows arched daintily over almond-shaped, olive-black eyes. Her light golden flesh gleamed as smooth and unblemished as Spanish polychromed tiles. Her features were delicately cut, except for her full-lipped, sensuous mouth. Her throat was a slender column, and her low-cut, lacy bodice accented the golden rise of full, high-standing breasts.

Longarm watched them approach, awed in spite of himself. The daughter seemed not to see them standing beside the coach; they simply didn't exist in her word. The father saw them, but showed no enthusiasm. He held his regal head erect, faintly aloof and withdrawn, without being discourteous. He was, in fact, icily polite. The *gringos* could expect nothing more from them.

Their servants stowed their baggage atop the coach, while the Don supervised silently. Then he smiled faintly at his daughter and nodded toward the coach. She smiled back and gathered her skirts above her ankles when he touched her elbow to help her enter the tonneau of the carriage.

"Señor Salazar. Señorita Salazar." Meriman's voice stopped them. "Meet our other passenger, Mr. Custis Long. Don Hernán Jorge Cortéz Salazar and his daughter—I regret, Doña Fernanda, I don't know *your* full name."

Doña Fernanda Maria Louisa Carlotta Salazar," Don Hernán said in a barely civil tone, still gently touching her elbow. "If you will permit us to enter. *Gracias.*"

Doña Fernanda settled herself in the plush seat facing forward at the other end of the seat where John Chisum sprawled, head back, eyes faintly amused. Her father sat between them, rigid, as if at attention.

Meriman winked at Longarm and swung up into the coach. He sat facing Chisum. Longarm got in beside Meriman and found himself gazing directly into Señorita Sal-azar's black, deep, unaware eyes. She stared through him, around him, over and past him, but he never once caught her even covertly looking *at* him.

Tom-Tom slammed the door, folded up the metal step, and levered himself up on the boot. The coach rocked gently for a moment and then rolled out of the yard as if riding on velvet.

Longarm sank back, luxuriating after the cramped torture of the old stage south from Denver. Without invading Doña Fernanda's space, he could stretch out his legs. He exhaled heavily, hoping against hope for a quiet trip.

From the moment the coach pulled out of Socorro and headed west, they could see the Black Range like a fringe of jagged black turrets. Once in a while, a white streak would shoot upward through the black faults. These were the only breaks in the high-flung formation. Not a tree or any vegetation showed on the high tors of those barren granite peaks. A few places were shattered at the head of a stream, or black crevices ripped through the forests of fir, spruce, and pine at lower levels. Or, infrequently, a snow-capped peak wore a yellow-leaf aspen like a single jaunty feather.

"Looks barren, don't it?" Meriman nodded toward the distant hills reared against the vermillion sky. "But I can assure you, Mr. Long, from Cookes Peak all the way north—one hundred and twenty-five miles in length and twelve miles across—that's the richest danged ground on the face of God's earth."

Something tapped against Longarm's boot and he jerked his head up, certain that Doña Fernanda Salazar had kicked him covertly, as if they shared some secret joke on the millionaire mine operator.

The ceramic-glazed smoothness of that lovely face remained aloof, remote, unaware of him.

He exhaled, chalking up the faint tap of the silver-tipped slipper as accidental. But now he was more aware of her than ever, able to yank his gaze from her, but not his heated thoughts.

179

"Had a few killings in Grant County over the last few months, Longarm," John Chisum began.

"And there will be more, Señor Chisum." Don Hernán Salazar's chilly, precise voice slashed across the rancher's.

"There have been a few cases of fellows letting daylight through one another in downtown Silver City," Meriman said, shrugging. "Don't mean anything—just a couple of citizens full of tarantula juice."

"It's more than that, and you know it, W. W.," Judge McLoomis said. "Silver City is unlike most mining towns—or always was, until now. It was built by men who meant for it to last, not to turn into another ghost town like Shakespeare or Chloride. These killings have been cold-blooded and premeditated—and most of them have been committed by hired, professional gunslingers."

"Nobody has been able to prove that, Judge," Meriman said in his mild voice.

"It will be proved," Judge McLoomis said. His voice was restrained, but quavered with suppressed emotion.

"Maybe you have some interest in these killings, Longarm?" Chisum suggested, watching Longarm narrowly.

"Don't know anything about all this." Longarm saw that this dialogue was like something planned to draw him into the discussion of the bloody troubles erupting in the mining town. It was the quickest way they knew to find out which side of the fence he was on. One thing was certain: he was caught between two mortally opposed camps in this plush carriage.

Longarm shrugged. "Like I say, none of this is in my bailiwick. Unless some government official is killed, murder is a local matter."

Don Hernán nodded his leonine head. "As it should be, *señor*. As it should be. The federal government refused to help us when Grant County wanted to annex itself to Arizona. We asked then only to be freed from domination by the Santa Fe Ring. Washington would not aid us then, let them keep their hands off now."

Longarm nodded. He knew that the Santa Fe Ring, although long since broken, hadn't yet died in the memories of many who lived in these parts. In fact, the last time he'd been in New Mexico Territory, he'd come down to follow up a suspicion that the notorious Ring had been revived to extort money from the new railroad that was laying track west from the territorial capital. At this moment, however, he decided to keep his mouth shut and listen to what the others had to say about it, and maybe pick up a few clues as to exactly how the sides in the present matter were being drawn up.

"What the Don refers to is—" Judge McLoomis began.

"Ancient history," Meriman said.

"The Spanish Grant titles," Judge McLoomis continued. "All this country was once part of Doña Ana County. Doña Ana, according to Spanish maps, included all land west of the Rio Grande to the California line. This included all the territory acquired by the United States in the Treaty of Guadalupe Hidalgo in 1848. Creation of the Arizona Territory in 1863 cut off all of Doña Ana County west of the thirty-second meridian, and those of us in what has become Grant County wished to annex ourselves to Arizona to escape the Santa Fe crooks, who are held in certain special interests' pockets. Let's say the people holding Spanish titles figured they'd fare better as part of Arizona Territory—"

"A sad fact which has been demonstrated a hundred times, proving that we were right," Don Hernán cut in. "We wanted to escape dishonorable and greedy exploiters. And we sit now at the mercy of rapacious mining interests—men who kill us when we protest their greed."

"Now just a cotton-pickin' minute, Don Hernán," Meriman said, grinning coldly in a way that made him look sinister and deadly behind his smiling. "We miners are just businessmen like you. Businessmen trying to get along. That's all."

Again, that silver-tipped slipper bumped lightly but surely against Longarm's sensitive instep.

His head jerked up. There was no mistaking the touch. He wore low-heeled cavalry stovepipe boots that were more suited for running than riding, and he paid extra to have

181

them made of soft calf's leather because he spent as much time afoot as he did in the saddle; these boots were lightweight and comfortable and fit him like a second layer of skin. Also, the road was level, the ride smooth, with little jostling compared to ordinary conveyances.

His mouth sagged slightly. When he glanced at Doña Fernanda, he found her serene face expressionless and bland. She seemed unaware of him. And she seemed, too, to have collected all the light in the cab about her. Even the gold cross on its fragile golden chain about her throat glittered and winked at him.

Holding his breath, Longarm decided to play her game. He inched his boot over and laid it gently against her slipper. Her reaction was instantaneous. The tiny foot was yanked away, though the gorgeous face remained cool and impassive.

Longarm withdrew his foot. Hell, he was too old to play footsie with a girl, anyway. He was a federal lawman, not a callow youth. He would put the aloof *señorita* out of his mind. He liked women, and she was the loveliest of females. But he wasn't desperate, not even for a magnificent nymph like this. To hell with her.

He was aware that a heated, though carefully modulated and courteous argument was raging between the four men.

Strange as hell! Getting odder by the minute. These four men, he knew, were principals in the violent belligerence bubbling in the cauldron of Chloride Flats. Yet these disputants—whose very lives depended on the outcome of this struggle—kept their voices civil and restrained—a hell of a lot more civilized than the statesmen wrangling over per diem in the Colorado assembly.

"The New Mexico Territorial Legislature must pass the Anti-Hydraulic Mining Act. *En nombre de Dios*, they must," Don Hernán said emphatically.

"They will," Chisum said with cool certainty. "Hell, it's the only kind of protection that will keep you Grant County ranchers and farmers in business."

Meriman laughed. "Gentlemen, gentlemen. A little reason. Please. There's no chance of that law's passing, now or later." He put his head back, laughing. "The law's evil, discriminatory, and unconstitutional. And as long as I've got a dime left to buy me some politicians, I'll hire the best that money can buy—and I'll fight you people for my constitutional rights."

"*Your* constitutional rights, W. W.?" Judge McLoomis said in a mild, sad tone. "What about the rights of others?"

"They'll have to get some crooked politicians and protect their own rights," Meriman said, laughing.

"That's a very cynical charge to make, W. W.," the judge protested. "Not every politician is crooked."

"Maybe not." Meriman smiled and shook his head. "But all of them I've ever met are for sale. Usually the price is right, so I can buy the best. And that's why, gentlemen, I guaran-damn-tee you that your blasted Anti-Hydraulic Mining Act won't get off the floor."

"It had better," Don Hernán Salazar said. "Or you miners will face an uprising of outraged ranchers and farmers and decent ordinary people that will make nightmares of your best days."

The atmosphere crackled with tension inside the swank coach, but Longarm, remembering what Marshal Billy Vail had said when he assigned him to this case the other day in Denver, knew that right had to crouch, scared to lift its head, somewhere between these two bellicose camps.

And then, suddenly, he felt that soft, insistent pressure of a slipper against the inside of his boot. It was hard to think about Billy Vail, or even to care about Billy Vail, with that kind of action going on.

He sucked in a deep breath and gazed across the seat toward Doña Fernanda. The lovely lady gazed quietly out the window, seemingly entranced by the sun-blasted wasteland of cactus and sage.

LONGARM

He's a man's man, a ladies'
man—the fastest lawman
around. Follow Longarm through all his shoot-'em-up
adventures as he takes on the outlaws—and the ladies-
of the Wild, Wild West!

_____ 05983-8	LONGARM #1	$1.95
_____ 05984-6	LONGARM ON THE BORDER #2	$1.95
_____ 05899-8	LONGARM AND THE AVENGING ANGELS #3	$1.95
_____ 05972-2	LONGARM AND THE WENDIGO #4	$1.95
_____ 06063-1	LONGARM IN THE INDIAN NATION #5	$1.95
_____ 05900-5	LONGARM AND THE LOGGERS #6	$1.95
_____ 05901-3	LONGARM AND THE HIGHGRADERS #7	$1.95
_____ 05985-4	LONGARM AND THE NESTERS #8	$1.95
_____ 05973-0	LONGARM AND THE HATCHET MAN #9	$1.95
_____ 06064-X	LONGARM AND THE MOLLY MAGUIRES #10	$1.95
_____ 05902-1	LONGARM AND THE TEXAS RANGERS #11	$1.95
_____ 05903-X	LONGARM IN LINCOLN COUNTY #12	$1.95
_____ 06153-0	LONGARM IN THE SAND HILLS #13	$1.95
_____ 06070-4	LONGARM IN LEADVILLE #14	$1.95
_____ 05904-8	LONGARM ON THE DEVIL'S TRAIL #15	$1.95
_____ 06104-2	LONGARM AND THE MOUNTIES #16	$1.95
_____ 06154-9	LONGARM AND THE BANDIT QUEEN #17	$1.95
_____ 06155-7	LONGARM ON THE YELLOWSTONE #18	$1.95

Available at your local bookstore or return this form to:

JOVE/BOOK MAILING SERVICE
P.O. Box 690, Rockville Center, N.Y. 11570

Please enclose 50¢ for postage and handling for one book, 25¢
each add'l book ($1.25 max.). No cash, CODs or stamps. Total
amount enclosed: $_____ in check or money order.

NAME_____

ADDRESS_____

CITY_____STATE/ZIP_____
Allow six weeks for delivery.

SK-5

LONGARM

Men love his rip-roaring, shoot-'em-up adventures...

Women delight in his romantic exploits!

This sexy lawman is as adventurous with the ladies as he is with his gun! Explore the exciting Old West with one of the men who made it wild!

05905-6	LONGARM IN THE FOUR CORNERS #19	$1.95
05931-5	LONGARM AT THE ROBBER'S ROOST #20	$1.95
05906-4	LONGARM AND THE SHEEPHERDERS #21	$1.95
06156-5	LONGARM AND THE GHOST DANCERS #22	$1.95
05999-4	LONGARM AND THE TOWN TAMER #23	$1.95
06157-3	LONGARM AND THE RAILROADERS #24	$1.95
05974-9	LONGARM ON THE OLD MISSION TRAIL #25	$1.95
06103-4	LONGARM AND THE DRAGON HUNTERS #26	$1.95
06158-1	LONGARM AND THE RURALES #27	$1.95
05584-0	LONGARM ON THE HUMBOLDT #28	$1.95
05585-9	LONGARM ON THE BIG MUDDY #29	$1.95
05587-5	LONGARM SOUTH OF THE GILA #30	$1.95
05586-7	LONGARM IN NORTHFIELD #31	$1.95
05588-3	LONGARM AND THE GOLDEN LADY #32	$1.95
05589-1	LONGARM AND THE LAREDO LOOP #33	$1.95
05590-5	LONGARM AND THE BOOT HILLERS #34	$1.95
05592-1	LONGARM AND THE BLUE NORTHER #35	$1.95
05591-3	LONGARM ON THE SANTE FE #36	$1.95

Available at your local bookstore or return this form to:

JOVE/BOOK MAILING SERVICE
P.O. Box 690, Rockville Center, N.Y. 11570

Please enclose 50¢ for postage and handling for one book, 25¢ each add'l book ($1.25 max.). No cash, CODs or stamps. Total amount enclosed: $_____ in check or money order.

NAME_____

ADDRESS_____

CITY_____STATE/ZIP_____

Allow six weeks for delivery.   SK-4